Tatematsu Wahei (1947-2010) received the Waseda Literary Prize for New Writers for *Jitensha* (*Bicycle*) while he was still a student. After graduating, he worked in a wide range of jobs before finding employment in local government in his home town of Utsunomiya City in 1973. While employed there, he continued to write and finally became a full-time author in 1979, publishing award-winning novels such as *Distant Thunder* and *Dogen Zenji*. A noted traveller and environmentalist, Tatematsu Wahei died in 2010.

Philip Gabriel published his first translation, a short story by Murakami Haruki , in 1988, and since then he has translated many of Murakami's works as well as novels by Oe Kenzaburo, Kuroi Senji, Shimada Masahiko, Yoshida Shuichi and Kirino Natsuo. He won the 2001 Japan–US Friendship Commission Prize for the translation of Japanese Literature, and in 2006 he was awarded the PEN/Book-of-the-Month Club Translation Prize for Murakami's *Kafka on the Shore*.

FROZEN DREAMS

FROZEN DREAMS

Based on a true story

TATEMATSU
Wahei

Translated by Philip Gabriel

PETER OWEN
London and Chicago

PETER OWEN PUBLISHERS
81 Ridge Road, London N8 9NP

Peter Owen books are distributed in the USA and Canada by
Independent Publishers Group/Trafalgar Square
814 North Franklin Street, Chicago, IL 60610, USA

Translated from the Japanese *Hidaka*
Originally published in Japan by Shinchosha, Tokyo

English translation first published in Great Britain 2012 by
Peter Owen Publishers

ISBN 978-0-7206-1497-8

A catalogue record for this book is available from the British Library.

Printed and bound by CPI Group
(UK) Ltd, Croydon, CR0 4YY

This book has been selected by the Japanese Literature Publishing Project
(JLPP), an initiative of the Agency for Cultural Affairs of Japan.

日高

'Among the countless truths within us lie both life and death.'

– *Shobogenzo*, Dogen

KANNA KAMUI, one of the Ainu gods, wanted to see water flowing, so he rose from the sea, and the Saru River, which has its headwaters in Mount Poroshiri, came into being. The river was a huge living creature that came from the sea, climbing into the mountains.

Poroshiri, the highest peak in the Hidaka Range in Hokkaido, stood afar, beyond an endless chain of mountains, and the Saru River flowed between them, connecting them all. On top of Poroshiri was a broad sea, with seagulls, sea lions and forests of seaweed. Sea lions would occasionally follow the river downstream, and seaweed had been known to flow downstream as well. *Kamui*, the Ainu gods, hate it if people speak Japanese rather than Ainu in the mountains and if they talk about the secular world. From a great distance you can hear enormous waves breaking along this sea on top of the mountain, and if you climb up to a certain point you can catch a glimpse of white bears. But any human who sees these creatures will immediately be caught up by a violent wind and blown away like a leaf down to the base of the mountains.

As he skied along, Noboru Odagiri thought about these Ainu legends. The snow on the logging road was packed down nicely, and it was easy to ski. Driving snow flew down from the overcast sky. Noboru was the leader of a six-member party from his college mountaineering club, and he felt slightly uneasy. While three members were seniors experienced at climbing, the others included a woman, Yuko Hasegawa – a second-year Education major who had climbed mountains in winter once – and two first-year students, Keizo Doi, from the Literature Department, and Ichiro Aizu, an Economics major, both of whom were complete novices. They might have been in a climbing club in high school, but a fourteen-day mountain excursion like this was something they had never undergone. This spring expedition was an officially sanctioned activity of the club, so Noboru had filed an itinerary. If they had an accident he knew the club would immediately mobilize former members, recent graduates, who would form a rescue team that would remain on call until the group was back. In that sense, Noboru and the others had a responsibility, not just to themselves but to others, to complete their trip safely.

Noboru rested his weight on his front ski, then lifted the heel of his rear ski, drawing it forwards with the tip of his toes as it skimmed the snow. As the skis came even with each other he continued to lean forwards, sliding his rear ski ahead until the heel touched down again. If you shifted your weight too abruptly to the ski sliding forwards you might lose your balance. Keeping his centre of gravity low, he slowly shifted his weight from one ski to the other. Before long he was performing this movement smoothly, without thinking. His muscles had warmed up, and he was perspiring slightly. He looked back from time to time to check on the others, seeing that they were maintaining an even distance between one another.

The slope began to run gently downhill, and they came upon a small prefab building, an office used by construction crews, unoccupied since work was halted for the winter. Today was 12 March. The group had left Sapporo yesterday on the night train, arriving early this morning in Obihiro. After sleepless nights preparing for the trip, they had all slept well on the train, which wasn't crowded. They were met in Obihiro by a Mr Akasaka, a former member of the mountaineering club, who ran a dairy farm in the foothills of the Hidaka. Akasaka had given them a ride in his truck to the start of the track where the houses petered out. The spot wasn't exactly near Obihiro, but Akasaka was happy to do what he could to help members of his old club. The rice balls the group had brought were nearly frozen, but they managed to eat them. Noboru had listened to the weather report and graphed out a weather map for them. A front was moving through, but it didn't sound like the weather would turn too nasty, so he decided they could proceed. On a long trip like this, two whole weeks, they couldn't expect the weather to be fair all the time.

They rested for a moment, keeping their skis on, using the prefab building as a windbreak, and set off again before they got too cold. The Satsunai River was frozen, a white ribbon of snow. Everything was snow and ice, but Noboru had visited the area in summer for training and knew the topography. Then he had changed into special shoes designed for wading in mountain streams and had splashed up river through the flowing icy water, which felt wonderful. The river was wide and at times looked like it would turn into a raging torrent, but it split off at points into smaller branches that then rejoined the river. On both sides were stands of alpine alders. The strong sun filtered through the leaves, and the matatabi plants, the underside of the leaves white, fluttered in the breeze, beckoning him deeper into the woods. And then there were the evening cicadas. They were the northernmost cicadas in the country, he was told, and they were chirping on both sides of the river as it flowed through the woods, surrounding him in a wave of sound.

As Noboru skied along the frozen winter river, the anti-slip tape on the bottom of his skis was working well, and he was able to climb the gentle slope easily. The wind was the only sound he heard. Somewhere far away, deep in the forest, in branches far above, the wind was blowing, now strong, now backing off. Twisting, turning, now swirling in several directions, now blowing straight ahead, the wind played a variety of tones. The dark silver trunks of the alders, their leaves gone, looked like an anguished, suffering crowd. But to Noboru, everything around him was beautiful.

The snow was sucked into the dark woods as it fell. The forest was like a black hole. The snow at his feet was soft fresh powder. Maintaining a steady rhythm, Noboru climbed the gentle slope. Aizu, the first-year Economics major who had the least skiing experience, was just behind him. From his laboured breathing, Noboru could tell Aizu was struggling. This was just the start of the trail up into the Hidaka, and a slight, uphill slope, nothing hard at all. Downhill skiing was where things got tricky. Downhill separated the experienced from the novice, so Noboru always chose the shortest path and set out only after making sure the entire party was together. He raised his ski pole in his right hand and stood still. After checking that all the climbers were with him, he carried on. Bringing up the rear were the two older students, Tadao Ariga, a small, calm young man, and Ken Yanagisawa, his opposite, a large man who none the less moved quickly.

The snow continued to fall, and, as Noboru exhaled, it made his breath even whiter. The snow was by turns hard then gentle. The group might have entered a small valley, for the snow was coming straight down now. The flakes that struck his cheeks melted instantly and felt magical. Noboru found it strange how this sort of world, which was hard for people to enter, could be laid out before him like this, so vast and open. Many people were completely unaware that so many isolated spots of such beauty existed, and he and his party of six were quietly passing through just such a world.

The mountaineering club had officially dubbed this a spring mountain climbing expedition, but *winter* mountain climbing might be more accurate for this March outing. March to May is usually considered spring – hence the term 'spring mountain climbing' – but in March, in these northern reaches of Japan, the Hidaka Range was still in the grip of winter. The gear they had brought was by necessity winter gear. Their plan, to be nine days on the move with five days of rest, would take them from Kamisatsunai up the Satsunai River, from the confluence of the Junosawa (literally Stream No. 10, the tenth of a series of streams) to the ridge of the left bank of the Junosawa, where they would climb up the ridge and camp at the Namewakka confluence. That would be their base camp from where they would climb Mount Kamuiekuuchikaushi. They would then pass the summit of Esaomantottabetsu and set up a second base camp on Mount Kamui. From there they would ascend Mount Poroshiri. And then they would hike across the northeast ridge of Mount Kamui, descend to the Totsutabetsu River and come down from the mountains in Obihiro. This was the route they had planned. If they climbed it in summer, they would have to make their way pushing aside bushes where there were no paths and a lot of steep inclines, although overall Noboru wouldn't rate it an especially hard climb. Winter, however, was a different story. The bushes were buried beneath snow, and the struggle would be against the snow itself. They would have to be on the look-out for avalanches, too, because they would be helpless if an avalanche roared down on them while they were making their way up a stream. The mountaineering club traditionally adopted the tactic of climbing up streams, since it was less arduous than walking along a ridge and there was no fear of falling. The itinerary this time had been reviewed and approved by the club, so every precaution was being taken. Of course, there were always dangers associated with mountains in winter – that was one of the attractions of climbing – still, they had to do whatever it took to avoid risks. When the temperature rose, so did the possibility of an avalanche, so it was best to find a safe place to camp as early as possible in the afternoon.

The wind picked up or died down, depending on the direction of the valley. The wind whipped against Noboru's face, and whenever he opened his mouth he could feel the cold deep in his throat. He signalled for the group to halt and looked at his map. Ariga and Yanagisawa caught up with him and peered at it.

'We're on schedule,' said Yanagisawa, his eyelashes covered with snowflakes, their crystalline structure sparkling.

'Yeah. Now where should we set up camp?'

'Let's climb up a little more. Stream beds are avalanche highways,' Ariga said, echoing Noboru's own thoughts, and gazed up the snowy slope. The woods were a safe place to be, even when the river overran its banks, and these woods contained among the alpine alders several ancient elms, oaks and todomatsu pines, their black trunks covered with snow.

'I'll go on ahead to see if there's a good place to dig a snow hole. Wait here for a minute.'

Now it was Yanagisawa who had the same idea as Noboru. Noboru just happened to be the leader this time, but after climbing together for four years he, Ariga and Yanagisawa had the same reflexes when it came to mountains. Yanagisawa removed his skis and stood on top of the snow as he strapped on *wakanjiki* – traditional wooden snowshoes. As he stomped around to pack down the snow, snow slid down off his yellow parka.

'Be back before you know it.' He smiled and headed off into the forest.

Mountain men of old might have been just like him, Noboru thought. No matter how tough things got, Yanagisawa would silently persevere, and he would do anything for the sake of his friends. As Noboru watched him leave, he realized that the snow was deeper than he had thought. At first up to Yanagisawa's waist, it soon grew deeper. The slope was steep, and as he stuck his poles into the snow they vanished. With each step Yanagisawa had to pull a submerged foot out of the snow, drag it back, then swing it in a large arc into order to take a step forwards. From Noboru's vantage point this bow-legged gait looked comical, even though it was evidently hard going. Yet there was rhythm to the way Yanagisawa did it, and he seemed to be enjoying himself. That was his strong point. Yanagisawa soon disappeared into the trees, leaving behind a trail of deep prints. For a while, though, they could still hear his laboured breathing and the crunch of his snowshoes.

Noboru took out some snacks from his backpack and laid them out on the snow. He had prepared individual plastic bags of sweets, chocolate, jelly beans, dried fruit and the like and had distributed them to everyone. He popped a sweet into his mouth, put the cellophane wrapping back into in the plastic bag and stuffed it into his pack. Sweets in the mountains tasted completely unlike they did at home. Yuko had been watching Yanagisawa as he was subsumed into the forest, and when she turned her gaze Noboru detected a nervousness in her.

'It'll be fine,' he said, as calmly as he could. *What* would be fine, though, he really didn't know. 'Don't worry. It'll be OK.'

The tension in Yuko's eyes softened, but Noboru couldn't

interpret what that change in her expression meant. Did Yuko like him? Perhaps she preferred Yanagisawa? Or another guy altogether? Noboru couldn't say. He tried to keep his confused feelings inside and assume an understanding smile, the way he felt a leader should.

'How do you like the mountains in winter?' he asked, his voice so loud everyone could hear. 'I don't think there's any place more beautiful,' he went on, seeing his original intention to talk to her on an intimate level slip away, and it felt like he had skirted past a tricky spot.

'I can barely keep up. I don't have time to enjoy the scenery,' she replied.

I'm the one who doesn't have the time to enjoy looking at *you*, Noboru thought, but he kept that to himself.

'Have you ever seen so much snow?' Perhaps sensing the awkward moment, Ariga threw Noboru a lifeline, which Noboru grabbed.

'There's been a lot of snow this year,' he said. 'There've been accidents all over Japan. We'll have to be very careful.' His words gradually seemed more relaxed.

'Have you ever dug a snow hole?' Ariga asked the two younger students.

'I made a snow cave for fun when I was a child. A little one,' Doi said, his enthusiastic reply very much that of a junior member of the club.

'Where are you from again?'

'Akita.'

'So you're used to snow.'

'I am, although the snow back home is wetter and heavier.'

'Aizu, you're from Chiba?'

'Yes, that's right.'

'So you're not used to snow.'

'It frightens me.'

'Hold on to that feeling.'

'I will.'

Noboru listened to this conversation as if it were taking place far away. It had become a little darker, as if the snow clouds had thickened or perhaps blocked the sun. *It frightens me.* Aizu's words stayed with Noboru. Snow was indeed frightening, but it was precisely the challenge of snow itself that made the mountains in winter so exhilarating. If it were merely cold, probably no one would climb mountains in winter. And the snow made everything beautiful.

'Hellooo! *Hellooo*!'

Yanagisawa's voice rang out, sounding very distant.

'Hellooo! *Hellooo*!' Noboru shouted back. It felt less like he was calling out to Yanagisawa than that he was calling out to the *kamui*.

'Come on. Follow my footprints! And somebody bring my skis, OK?'

Yanagisawa's words were clear, so they knew he was close by.

'Right! We're coming!' Noboru shouted again. He untied his snowshoes from his pack and strapped them to the soles of his plastic climbing boots. Ariga unstrapped one of the skis, which Noboru shouldered along with his own. He checked the rest of his party then took off into the trees, again in the lead.

The branches of the ezo matsu firs and todomatsu pines

were covered with snow, but around the trunk of each tree there was clear space with enough room to sit and meditate. It was as if the space beneath each tree was a *dojo* for ascetic training. Only in winter, of course.

As the group made its way, they not only had to contend with the deep snow but with the steep slope. Even with Yanagisawa's footprints to step into it was rough going. Noboru placed a snowshoed foot down lightly, then pulled it back, rested a beat, then stepped forwards again. Keeping the shoes parallel to the ground was important, otherwise your weight wouldn't be distributed evenly. Since Noboru was on one foot most of the time he had to rely on his ski poles, thrust through the snow, to keep his balance. He stepped lightly at first so as to make the ice crystals in the snow adhere to each other, increasing their load-bearing properties. With each step he took, the snow beneath him made a teeth-gritting creak – all the while snow continued to fall and settle. Noboru felt almost overwhelmed by the intensity of it.

Apparently Yanagisawa was more afraid of avalanches than Noboru had realized. His path through the snow took them to much higher ground than he had expected. With the curtain of falling snow, however, he couldn't really determine where Yanagisawa was. Noboru finally found him on a kind of shelf in the woods, trudging back and forth to pack down the snow and prepare a place to pitch their tents. The other four members arrived at the spot, and at Yanagisawa's direction they set down their equipment, unstrapped their snowshoes, lined up abreast of one another and helped to damp down the ground. Noboru walked over to Yuko. Although she evidently had several layers underneath her anorak, he was acutely aware of her slender form, so very different from that of a man. They walked back and forth three times. The ground was now flat.

Yanagisawa and Aizu carried the tents. There was no wind, so it was easy to set them up. In a snowstorm this could be an agonizing task, with several people having to hold down the canvas as it lashed about in the wind, struggling to assemble the frame and secure the lines to pegs pounded into the snow. When there wasn't any wind, it was as simple as putting up a tent in a campsite in summer. Now, instead of pegs, the group stuck ice axes into the snow on three sides of the tent and fixed the lines tautly to them. These were three-man tents, and the two tents were pitched next to one another.

Since they were in a forest, it was easier to put tents up than to dig a snow hole. They had some time, so they decided to create a windbreak out of blocks of snow that they would stack around the bright-yellow tents, which stood out amid their white surroundings. From the flat area they had levelled they shovelled clumps of snow on the windward side of the tents. The snow on the trees had piled up on the leeward side, and they found it easy to use their snow saws to carve out blocks for the windbreak. The task was simpler since the wind was blowing up from the valley.

They set their skis beside the tents and tied down their poles and snowshoes so they wouldn't be blown away. They filled 45-litre bags with snow to use for water and placed them near the entrances of the tents. When they were ready to cook or wanted to make tea, all they had to do was reach outside the tent and grab some snow. They made a path to a spot to use as a latrine. Finally, they laid the shovels just outside the tents so they could reach them easily. Their outdoor work was now done.

The three senior students were to occupy one tent, the younger members the other. Brushing off the snow, Noboru stepped halfway into his tent where he undid the spats that served as leggings and removed the outer layer of his plastic hiking boots. Wearing the inner layer of his boots, he moved about the tent and arranged the backpacks on one side.

The tent, with three men in it, felt cramped, but the space was cosy and out of the wind. They spread a silver thermal mat over the entire floor of the tent, then blow-up mattresses on top of that. They laid out their sleeping-bags and on top of them the covers. They rolled up clothes to use as pillows. Next they stretched a rope across the ceiling on which to hang their gloves and socks and prevent them from freezing. That completed the sleeping arrangements. The younger students would be making dinner, but the others still had time for tea. They heaped snow into a pot, lit the stove and waited for the snow to turn into hot water.

'I wonder if they'll cook something decent,' Ariga said, motioning with his chin to the tent next door.

'They said they'd make beef and rice,' Yanagisawa said.

Being responsible for the cooking wasn't such a chore, although not having to prepare the food was certainly easier. The wind whistled far away. Maybe it was because of the windbreak or maybe it was because of the direction of the wind, but it wasn't blowing directly up against the tents.

This spot in the forest might have been the perfect place to camp. But if you came here in summer you would have to wade through butterbur and giant knotweed taller than you and trample through one muggy thicket after another that the wind never reached. There would be no reason to come here unless you were collecting *sansai*, edible forest plants.

'I wonder if they're afraid. It's going to get a lot tougher,' Ariga said, revealing what had been on his mind.

'Everyone's like that at first. I bet we were.'

'We've been climbing mountains in winter since high school.'

'The first time I climbed in winter it was terrifying.'

'I bet it was.'

'My parents were in tears, totally against it, and I was secretly ready to die if it came to it. It was only Tanzawa, in Kanagawa, though, an easy climb.'

'My first winter climb was Mount Adatara. There was even a hut with a hot springs. One of those iron huts.'

As he listened to his companions talk, Noboru took out a mechanical pencil and on a map of the area noted their present location with the words '12 March: camp'. In the pot on the stove, the chunk of snow started to bob like an iceberg, losing its whiteness as it melted. Nothing in this world stands still, Noboru thought. Everything is in constant motion. And people struggle to find quiet place in which to live.

Noboru switched on his head-torch and spread out his weather map. He turned on the radio, tuning into the weather channel; the announcer's voice faded in and out as he read the wind direction, wind speed, precipitation, air pressure and temperature. Noboru wrote it all down. The forecast began in southernmost Japan and moved northwards from Ishigaki-jima, Naha and Minami Daito-jima up through Honshu to Hokkaido – including Hakodate, Uraga, Nemuro and Wakkanai – then from the Kuril Islands and Sakhalin, turning south along the Coastal Range, the Korean peninsula, then from Taiwan over to the Chinese mainland and north to Changchun, then back south again to Hong Kong, Chichi-jima in the Ogasawara Islands, winding up with Mount Fuji. The broadcast took twenty minutes to cover the basic weather fronts in Japan. Noboru then connected the places with the same atmospheric pressure with a rough curved line. What he ended up with was an air-pressure distribution typical of winter weather patterns, namely high pressure in the west, low pressure in the east. Far west of Japan was a dominant mass of high pressure centred over Siberia, while a low pressure system had already developed in the Pacific, near the Kurils, northeast of Hokkaido. The group could expect a west wind from mainland Asia that would gradually increase to fill in the gap between the two pressure systems. Cold air was flowing in at a height of 5,500 metres, and moisture rising from the Tsushima Current would be chilled there and have to release its moisture. Strong wind and a heavy snowfall – a snowstorm, in other words – was the forecast for tomorrow. Noboru reported this to Ariga and Yanagisawa.

'Let's not push it. Sometimes in life you just need a little down time,' Yanagisawa said as he sipped his tea.

One teabag had made three cups. Noboru showed Yanagisawa the weather map and took a sip of tea as well. Fragrant steam rose up.

‘The day after we come down off the mountains I’m going to my parents’ place in Tokyo, then I’ll come back to Sapporo the day before my company’s entrance ceremony for new employees. I should have a week free in between. But if we get stuck up here too long and I don’t make to the ceremony, I hope the company won’t change its mind about hiring me.’ Noboru put the doubt that had been festering inside him into words.

Ariga, who had been promised a position at a television station in Sapporo, answered quickly. ‘They wouldn’t do that. Just explain what happened, and you’ll be OK.’

‘We only just got here. Some down time is built into our schedule,’ Yanagisawa laughed, although he felt uneasy. But this was the unease he always felt when he went into the mountains in winter. Putting yourself into this state of mind, which bordered on fear, was, after all, part of the appeal of winter climbing. Yanagisawa had a job lined up in the Hokkaido government. Once he started work he wouldn’t be able to take a long outing such as this, which is why he had signed up for this climb.

‘That’s nuts. No need to worry about something you knew about in advance. What I’m worried more about is why dinner’s late. I’m going to take a leak then go and check on how they’re doing,’ Yanagisawa said, still in a jocular tone. It was growing dark inside the tent, and without the light from head-torches you couldn’t see your hands. Yanagisawa put on his inner boots, unzipped the tent flap and went out, leaving the flap undone. Half the air in the tent was replaced by a rush of freezing air from outside. With Yanagisawa gone there was more room to move around. Ariga poured the remaining hot water into an aluminium canteen. He slipped it into the foot of his sleeping-bag where it would serve as a hot-water bottle. Also that way it wouldn't freeze overnight and could be reheated in the morning for tea. Before the teabag froze Noboru ripped it open, discarded the tea leaves and put the remaining rubbish in a plastic bag, which would be his personal bin bag to take with him away from the mountains.

'Hey! You can see the stars!' Yanagisawa's voice bellowed from outside. Noboru and Ariga quickly got up, but in his bulky clothes Noboru couldn't move freely, so he had to crawl out of the tent. He got to his knees and lifted up his eyes, the beauty of the sky taking his breath away. The backdrop to the leafless trees was the night sky, bathed in a silver glow, countless stars scattered like so much dust, looking like the true source of all light. Each dot was twinkling furiously, as if the whole blinking mass was the universe breathing. The wind had died away.

'Where am I?' Noboru heard Yuko say. He turned in the direction of her voice and saw her there, head-torch on, gazing up at the sky. The orange light from her forehead shone in a straight line to the sky. To Noboru it looked as if that light was reflecting off the stars.

'So tomorrow will be sunny?' Aizu asked

'No,' Noboru quickly replied. 'The atmosphere's unstable.'

To Noboru, the valley of the isobaric curve over the Pacific Ocean he had just pencilled into his weather map seemed like a bottomless abyss. And he felt as if he were gazing up now at the heavens from that abyss. The darkness surrounding the stars was so clear it seemed polished.

Noboru wasn't optimistic about the weather, but with a starlit sky like this the way should open up for them somewhere. What they had to do was to seek out that way patiently.

Around him, members of the party sighed. Suddenly fog rolled in, which closed off the stars, accompanied by a piercing wind. Noboru was reminded where he was – in the mountains in winter.

'Dinner's ready. Let's eat.'

Yuko's voice sounded clear and pure to Noboru. He fetched his mug, spoon and pot and entered the tent, which had two gas stoves going. Doi, sitting cross-legged beside the stoves, reached a gloved hand into the pot of hot water and extracted two plastic bags – one of rice, the other of beef – and placed them into Noboru's pot. Noboru tore open a small packet, poured the powder into his mug and added hot water. This made him a cup of wakame soup.

Noboru didn't hang around outdoors, or his food would have gone cold, so he went straight back into his tent. He tore open the heated plastic bags, made his beef and rice and dug into it with his spoon. With the head-torch he could see his food quite clearly. Not that he needed to – it was all standard fare. It tasted just like beef and rice, and nobody would argue otherwise. A hot meal in the mountains in winter was a real treat. The wakame soup was a bit strong and could do with more water, but it, too, tasted exactly the way it was supposed to. After he had finished eating Noboru asked Ariga for the canteen from Ariga's sleeping-bag and poured the hot water into his mug, poured that into his pot and scoured the pot with his spoon. Then he drank the liquid. He wiped his utensils, careful to use the toilet paper sparingly. He placed the rubbish into his personal bin bag.

Noboru took a drink of whisky from a canteen and passed it to Yanagisawa. Yanagisawa and Ariga each took a sip and passed it back to Noboru. They had many days to go, so they were rationing the whisky to one nip per person before bed. They didn't have to worry about the whisky freezing, so Noboru placed it in a corner of the tent. He stepped outside to pee. It was foggy and dark. His deed done, wearing a jacket, over-trousers and two pairs of socks, Noboru slipped into his sleeping-bag, over which was the cover, and then, for even more warmth, he stuck his sleeping-bag-wrapped legs into his emptied backpack. The down-filled sleeping-bag was warm, and Noboru felt happy, snug and comfortable even in the depths of these harsh winter mountains. No doubt tomorrow would be a happy day, too. From the way Yuko glanced at him, the gleam in her eye and something he couldn't quite describe about her demeanour, he was getting the signal that she had feelings for him. It was a little frustrating that the signals weren't clearer, but he was sure that during this trip they would reach some kind of resolution. Noboru was hoping that a relationship would develop out of this, which is why he had to be alert. He had to show her that he was a man she could depend on. He had not heard of anything between Yanagisawa and Yuko. Yanagisawa surely liked Yuko, but in the same way he liked Noboru, so Noboru could rest easy and just focus on the trip and the mountains ahead. Noboru smiled as he reached this conclusion and fell asleep. The happy feeling continued as he slept.

*

Wrapped in the warmth of his own body, Noboru woke up. He stretched out and folded his arms together at his chest. He reached for the head-torch near his pillow and shone it on his wristwatch, careful that the light didn't spill out. It was 3.30. He had slept long enough. Even if he fell asleep again he would have to get up in half an hour. He now shone his head-torch around the tent and saw that the ceiling was bowed, sagging under the weight of snow, so much so that the interior was reduced by a quarter. No wonder the air in the tent seemed stuffy.

Noboru unzipped his sleeping-bag and got dressed. Wearing his inner boots, he ventured outdoors. Snow immediately swirled into the tent. Someone's snoring – he couldn't tell whose – stopped. There was no wind, but the snow was coming down harder. He pulled on his over-gloves and zipped the tent up from the outside.

It was pitch black. He could only see as far as the circle of light from his head-torch. The tents were solid lumps of snow, two little snowy hillocks. If they turned on the stoves in the tents when they were like this they would get carbon monoxide poisoning immediately. Noboru took five steps away from the tent, peed, then grabbed the shovel standing in front of the younger students' tent. About thirty centimetres of snow had fallen overnight, a lot in such a short time. As long as the typical winter weather pattern continued – high pressure in the west, low pressure in the east – they were in for a real struggle with the snow.

Noboru shovelled the snow off the tent Yuko was in first. For a brief moment he pictured her asleep – her body tightly swathed inside her sleeping-bag, but under the many layers was soft, pliant flesh. He imagined himself unzipping her sleeping-bag and breathing in the fragrance of her body. In a couple of days I would like to work things out with her, he thought, then the rest of the climb will be fantastic. Snow had accumulated between the tent and the windbreaks of snow they had erected. After carefully digging it out, he tapped the top of the tent with the back of the shovel. The tent shook, and the snow slid off. A torch beam came on, briefly grazing the inside of the tent, but the stirring stopped and the light went out. Whoever it was must have seen that it was still early.

Noboru started removing the snow from his own tent, feeling less of a need to be careful. After tapping the top of the tent a couple of times, he could see the yellow of the fabric again. It felt like the tent was breathing.

'Noboru? Sorry I didn't help,' he heard Ariga saying from inside the tent.

'Hey, no problem,' Noboru said, shovelling the snow that had fallen between the tent and the windbreak. Whoever noticed that shovelling was needed did it. With each shovelful, the powdery snow spread out in the darkness. Since there was no wind, the windbreak blocks hadn't helped at all. They had actually made the snow pile up more around the tents.

In the windless darkness the snow kept tumbling down. It was amazing that this much could fall. It was snowing so hard that Noboru grew anxious. If the wind picked up, this could turn into a serious snowstorm. Their world was hovering on the edge of collapse, and it wouldn't take much to push it over the edge. Noboru gazed up at the sky, unable to rid himself of this foreboding. The snow fell right into his wide-open eyes, like freezing fingers poking his eyeballs. He closed his eyes.

The breakfast menu consisted of ramen with mochi rice cakes. While the food was prepared, Ariga melted snow to make water. He filled a pan with snow, added some water to help melt it and placed the pot on top of the stove. He stirred the snow to break it apart, which made it melt even faster. This was the water they would put in the canteens and use for that day.

Noboru and Yanagisawa studied the weather map and discussed the situation with Ariga as he continued to melt the snow. It was over four hours before the next radio weather report. There was no doubt they were in a typical winter weather pattern, and it was a good bet that the extreme pressure difference would lead to strong winds. The question was how bad it was going to get.

'Isn't there a risk of avalanches if we stay in the stream bed?' Noboru said.

'There's more risk if we climb up the ridge,' Yanagisawa replied.

'Climbing up, wading through the deep snow, isn't easy,' Ariga added as he transferred snow from one pot to another.

'I guess the main thing is to make sure we all come out alive,' Noboru said. He felt slightly put off by Yanagisawa, whom he thought was overly concerned about risk, although Noboru was aware of the difficulties ridge-climbing would pose for three novices, one of whom was a woman.

'Of course. But there won't be any avalanches while it's still snowing.'

'Still, I wonder how much overhang there is.'

Overhang was the accumulated snow on the brow of a mountain that was blown downwind by seasonal winds. When it collapsed, it became an avalanche. Noboru felt uncomfortable with how blasé Ariga was.

'The seasonal winds on the Hidaka Range are mostly from the west, and the overhangs project in the direction of Tokachi. The Satsunai River is on the eastern part of the Hidaka. If overhangs develop it's possible that they could fall apart and cause an avalanche. So I think we need to get out of this stream as soon as we can. If we get to the Junosawa confluence some time today then we can make it. Anyhow, let's get out of this stream.'

Noboru stated this firmly, but he was still uneasy. He was always uneasy in the mountains in winter because you never knew what could happen. When it came to climbing, nothing was absolutely certain. Since Noboru, the group leader, had made his case firmly, the issue was settled.

'Since that's decided, let's get ready to go. If we keep debating, we won't get anywhere,' Noboru spoke roughly in order to forestall further discussion.

The food was ready, and they ate. When Noboru left the tent the wind had started to blow. The snow was falling at a slight angle. The junior members of the group packed away the food and cookware and readied themselves to go.

'OK! Let's get moving!' Noboru shouted, snow flying into his mouth. The younger students began to dismantle their tent immediately. Ariga and Yanagisawa undid the guys of their tent, which had been tied to a tree. When Noboru dismantled the aluminium frame the tent collapsed. He carefully brushed off the snow, folded it and stowed it in Yanagisawa's backpack. Climbing in winter also meant heavy equipment and restricted movement.

Noboru was still unsure which was better, to climb up the glen or to traverse the mountainside in order to lessen the likelihood that they would run into an avalanche. Traversing the mountain on skis in fresh snow required skill. Since Aizu had little experience with skis he decided they should climb up the glen. That was their original plan, so there was no need for him to say anything. He strapped on his skis, and the others silently followed suit. Aizu was slow at getting his on.

'It might be hard going. Yuko will follow me. Then Aizu. Then Doi. Ariga and Yanagisawa will bring up the rear.'

Noboru spoke briskly, as he felt a leader should, and looked at Yuko. Under her knit cap and hood her eyes seemed to smile. This was the faint signal she seemed to like to send him. That meaningful smile. So the others wouldn't notice, at the last instant before he started to look away, he shot her a quick smile. It felt like two sharp blades crossing each other.

He began skiing, moving around the trees. Fifty centimetres of light, soft, powdery snow had accumulated overnight. Since there had been no wind when the snow fell, the snow crystals were intact, each flake a beautiful, dendritic hexagon. When the surface was flat, a smooth layer of ice crystals, it was easier to ski. Easier to ski but also easier for avalanches to occur. When the wind blew, the crystals broke apart as the snow fell, wedging themselves between the crystals of fallen snow, compacting the snow. The wind was now whipping between the trees.

In the snow, each tree, even the large ones, seemed short. Without their leaves, Noboru couldn't tell what kind of trees they were. Occasionally he could see the peak of the mountain beyond the valley. In the wall of snow, the trees appeared washed out, like an India-ink drawing, rough and detailed at the same time. He looked up at the scenery then back down at his feet as he continued skiing. When he looked up again, the mountain was gone, covered in snow clouds. Forgetting for a moment that they were surrounded by peaks, Noboru skied around trees, rhythmically kicking forwards through the snow. With nylon brush seals on their bottom these skis didn't slide all that well. The fresh powder was soft and made the skis sink. Keeping his eye on those behind him, he made a long curve off the path and blazed a new trail through the snow. Yuko's laboured breathing caught up to him. His body had warmed up, and he was perspiring lightly.

Each time Aizu fell, Doi yelled. Noboru immediately discarded the mental image of where he would go and at what angle and came to a halt, his skis flat against the snow.

'It must be tough for you.' With his skis pointed forwards, Noboru twisted around and spoke to Yuko, who was right behind him. He didn't care if the others found out that he liked her. After he graduated it would be hard for them to see each other, and time was short. As he saw Yuko's generous smile he was glad the sun wasn't shining and she didn't have her sunglasses on.

'I'm enjoying myself.'

'If it wasn't enjoyable, nobody would put up with all this hardship,' Noboru said. For this brief moment it was he and Yuko, just the two of them.

'I really am having a good time,' she said, her healthy white teeth showing.

In the mountains in winter it was a hassle to brush one's teeth, but Noboru was sure that Yuko was brushing hers every day. I'll be sure to brush mine tonight, he thought. 'I guess if you think something's a hardship then it's going to be,' he said.

Just as Noboru spoke Aizu appeared, covered in snow, from the shadow of a tree, going too fast. Noboru had to halt his conversation with Yuko as he watched Aizu overshoot his tracks and fall yet again.

'Sorry!' Aizu yelled as he fell. The snow was deep, and he almost disappeared into it. Doi came up after him, held out a ski pole to him and pulled him to his feet. It took a while, and the others had to wait for them.

'There's no need to rush. If you use too much energy you'll wear yourself out.'

If he kept this up, Aizu would wind up being a drag on them. When we head up the slope it might be better to carry my skis and wade through the snow, Noboru thought as he watched Aizu get to his feet, brush off the snow and make his way towards him.

The wind whipped around each tree, the snow steadily grew heavier, and it looked like the trees were connecting the sky to the ground. There was no vista ahead, so all they knew about was where they stood. Even without consulting a compass or a map they would run into the Satsunai River as long as they headed down. If they went in a straight line they would hit the river right away, but they might be coming in at too shallow an angle.

Noboru deliberately chose a gentle slope to make it easy for Aizu, carefully avoiding the clumps of snow that had accumulated along the way. Aizu didn't fall again for a while, so they were able to continue at a good pace. Their skis whooshed across the snow.

They reached the Satsunai River. Noboru had hiked up it any number of times in summer, but it was incomparably easier in winter. The numerous undulations in summer were now a simple flat path of snow. As far as he could see, there was no debris from an avalanche – any accumulation of rocks, mud and trees that an avalanche brought down with it. Noboru took the lead and skied down the soft, pure-white fresh snow. Is the water below still running? he wondered. He stood above the river and waited for the rest of the party to emerge from the woods. While he was in the woods the trees had seemed sparse, but now, looking back, he saw a dense forest. The river wasn't wide, but the falling snow hid the forest on the other bank.

'You OK?' Noboru said this everyone in the party, but he was looking at Yuko.

'We're OK. Everybody's fine,' Yuko answered for the others, her words a slight criticism of Noboru. The leader of any party into the mountains was strictly forbidden to show favouritism. This was the hard-and-fast rule.

'Good,' Noboru said simply and turned to look at the rest

of the line of climbers. Noboru knew clearly that Yuko was fully aware of him. Her subtle tone of voice was a signal to him.

'Is everybody doing OK?' Noboru called out to the last in line.

'We're fine.' Yanagisawa's voice filtered back to Noboru, wavering slightly in the wind.

High above on the peaks, the wind was roaring. We could be in for a snowstorm, Noboru thought.

'Let's make up some ground. But, Aizu, I don't want you to overdo it. If you're having a hard time, give me a yell, OK? Don't push it.'

He kicked off with his skis and set off again. Put too much weight on the front foot all at once and your movement would be clumsy. The trick was to shift your weight steadily so it feels as if your weight is always on your hips. Repeat this movement mechanically, and over time it all becomes automatic.

This snowy road led to the peak of Poroshiri, the land of Kanna Kamui. Here the gods dwelled as white bears. In the winter sea in the divine land, where humans never approached, sea lions lived in carefree innocence. As soon as Noboru and the others set foot there the land of the *kamui* would crumble. So in the end, humans like Noboru and his group would never be able to meet Kanna Kamui. Not in this lifetime anyway.

Kanna Kamui might be playing near the top of Poroshiri, while black bears were asleep in their caves.

They had to follow a single wide trail so they wouldn't get lost. The only thing to fear here was an avalanche. The group had no choice but to keep going, because if an avalanche struck they would be buried.

On the left side as they went up, the streams flowed down from Mount Kamuiekuuchikaushi and Mount Shunbetsu to join the Satsunai River. The streams are numbered, the numbers increasing as you go higher, thus Stream No. 8, Stream No. 9, Stream No. 10 . . . Last night they camped a little upstream from the confluence of Stream No. 8 and the river. Today they wanted to climb past Stream No. 9 and make camp around the confluence of Stream No. 10, Junosawa. If they climbed up to the ridge on the left bank they should be safe from avalanches. It was best that they get out of the danger zone as quickly as possible.

The wind was striking them from the front, so Noboru ordered a short break and used the time to get everyone to put on their goggles. He noticed Yuko eating something and popped a sweet into his mouth. As he moved his tongue around it, the hard sweet made a pleasant clicking as it struck the back of his teeth. They would get cold if they stayed put for long, so Noboru set off again. He raised the hood of his jacket and zipped the collar up to his chin. The snow hit his goggles at tremendous speed, breaking apart before blowing away. The snow didn't let up. It was like some infinite passion – passion of a malicious nature.

Noboru was heading directly into the wind, and it nearly blew him off his feet, making him stagger. He was in the lead and had to shelter the others from the wind, so he had to hold on, and he soon found himself breathing heavily. He got the group to close ranks, then made Ariga take the lead while he brought up the rear. He was behind

Yanagisawa now, and the wind was much easier to handle. The wind blowing from deep in the valley stirred up the snow on the ground, causing it to swirl into its own miniature snowstorm. There was no sign of the snow letting up. With high winds and poor visibility this was turning into a bad storm.

It had got worse so quickly Noboru was hoping that it might subside just as suddenly. He called for breaks every fifteen minutes, but when they squatted down to rest the swirling snow made it impossible to breathe. So they turned their backs to the wind and stood there, resting on their poles. No one spoke. If you opened your mouth snow would blow in.

Noboru was perplexed. He glanced at his watch and saw it wasn't quite 9 a.m. He wanted to make up ground, but if they forced themselves forwards they would be exhausted. Maybe it would be best to dig a snow hole and bivouac here. But he was afraid to stop where they stood. Better to climb far up the side of the mountain to find a safer place. The wind twisted and chafed, making a sound almost like a scream. Noboru called over Yanagisawa and Ariga, and they huddled together to discuss the situation.

'I think we need to find a place to dig a snow cave,' Noboru said emphatically to mask his vacillating feelings.

'The weather turned nasty so fast it's hard to tell what it's going to do. Let's find somewhere out of the wind for now,' Ariga said, not thinking they needed to make a decision yet.

'I can't take out my map,' said Yanagisawa, 'but if I remember right the Satsunai River makes a ninety-degree turn to the left just up ahead. If we go straight we'll hit the

Kinen Stream. The Satsunai flows west, so maybe the wind direction will change. The valley gets way narrower up there. If there's a strong wind we won't be able to go on, but there's a good chance there won't be any.'

Yanagisawa was urging them to grit their teeth and press on. Once again Noboru was standing between these two men and their opinions. But that's what made him the leader. In Noboru's mind Yanagisawa made the more persuasive case. He couldn't help wondering how Yuko would react to Yanagisawa's idea, but he knew that as group leader he couldn't let personal feelings play any part in the decision. Yuko was smart, and Noboru knew she would understand why he chose that path.

'Yanagisawa's right. Let's go on a little more,' Noboru said, patting both men on the back simultaneously. This was not the time to show any hesitation. 'OK, let's move out! We'll go a bit further,' he called out to the group, the cold air going down his throat as he inhaled. The wind was rasping above him, but it seemed the sound was inside his throat.

Yanagisawa took the lead. When the going got tough Yanagisawa was the man for the job. Ariga was cautious to the point of being passive, and Yanagisawa was the exact opposite, going on the offensive no matter the circumstances. He forged on into the driving wind and snow, using his body to shield the others from the wind. The snow was flying almost horizontally. It struck their goggles and broke into powder.

Noboru took the lead again. The wind whipped across his chest and stomach, and his skis felt like they were being pushed backwards. He crouched lower and stumbled forwards, his chin pulled in, his forehead out. It felt like he was leaning against a white wall on the verge of collapsing on top of him. No individual flakes were visible. It was coming down in clumps, and the group was right in the middle of it. Noboru couldn't make out anything around him. This was a white-out.

Noboru just struggled on in the direction they had agreed. He couldn't see his own skis or judge if they were moving up or down. The breathing from behind him was Yuko's. It was a kind of road marker for him, when all around him was solid white. He thought it was because snow was clinging to his goggles, and he wiped them off repeatedly, but nothing changed. He continued at the same grinding pace, thinking that if they couldn't wait the blizzard out it was the only thing they could do. Like Yanagisawa said, the river turns, so the wind direction should change, too. No matter what, he reasoned, if we stick to the river, we won't get lost. And in this gale the snow crystals will break apart, and small fragments will get mixed in, filling the gaps between the large crystals. So the snow will accumulate densely and compactly. Danger of a surface avalanche was minimal. The situation was much safer than it looked.

Noboru raised his right hand and turned around. He felt like he was about to be blown over from behind. Someone's vague outline was in front of him, but he couldn't see who it was. From the breathing, though, he knew it was Yuko.

'We need the climbing rope,' he called out. He didn't have to yell, for the wind was carrying his voice. 'Yanagisawa, pass the rope from the rear. Everybody, attach the rope to your harness. I don't want anyone getting lost in this.'

Yanagisawa was carrying a rope seven millimetres in diameter and fifty metres in length. Noboru couldn't see from where he was, but it was Ariga who took the rope out of Yanagisawa's backpack. Yanagisawa had on a waist harness, and he tied the rope to its metal catch, making a figure of eight. Noboru pictured Ariga passing the rope to Doi, and then to Aizu, and then to Yuko, but when he expected the rope to get to him it wasn't there. The wind was slowing down the process. Noboru made his way over to Yuko, standing beside her so he wouldn't step on her skis. Still no rope. He went back to Aizu, who was struggling with it. Removing his gloves, Noboru tied the rope to the aluminium snap on his harness for him. Then he unravelled the rope about eight metres and tied it to Yuko's harness.

'We could end up stranded,' Yuko said in a small voice. It was definitely her voice, but to Noboru it sounded like another woman.

'That won't happen,' he said. 'Why do you think so?' Even at a tense time like this it made him happy to be able to talk with her.

'Because we've been unlucky. The weather's getting worse.'

'This is nothing.'

'I have a bad feeling about this,' Yuko said. 'I have a sixth sense about things.'

'That'll never happen. This storm can't last for ever.' Noboru laughed slightly as he tied the rope to his own harness. As he touched the aluminium catch his fingertips grew numb. He pulled on his gloves, made the leftover rope into a loop and hung it from his waist.

'I don't mind being stranded – since I'm with you.'

The moment he heard her say these words, a sense of unease ran through him Noboru, and he drew back. Yuko smiled, her eyes sparkling as an entirely different atmosphere surrounded the two of them. This was the signal he had been waiting for, and Noboru felt the tug of temptation. This quiet yet unexpectedly intense expression of her feelings threw him. Now, even the blizzard looked beautiful. Most likely no one else had seen the expression on his face, but, unsure what to do, he erased the look he had given her.

'I feel the same,' he finally was able to say. As the words left his lips, they were blown off by the wind, as if they were carried along not just to her but to everyone else. A thick wall of snow blew up cutting off all visibility. Maybe that's a good thing, he thought, for now Yuko, close by him, couldn't see his face. He turned back into the wind with a happy, contented smile. He forged on ahead with all his strength. The rope pulled against his waist, weight tugging at the harness of his belt. When the rope grew taut he halted and, still facing forwards, shouted, 'Let's head on out!'

A weight pulled at him from behind. It was like a sign from Yuko telling him she was there. He could picture her dazzling smile. Nothing around him could compare with its brightness. Yuko soon began moving on her own, and there was no more weight tugging at him. Using only one pole as he made his way, Noboru took the compass out of his pocket. He had to bring it right up to his face to read it.

Since he was moving the needle wavered, but he could make out the four directions. According to the map that was burned into his memory, they were on the right course. He slid a ski forwards, leaning ahead from the waist, his legs performing this motion alternately. His poles pierced the snow smoothly, naturally, propelling him onwards. Noboru was conscious of his body movement, but soon his arms and legs began to move in a rhythm. In his mind Yuko's smile grew more and more dazzling. It was still a white-out, but to the side the shapes of trees were just visible. They were like milestones. The wind blowing in his face bothered him, but for the most part he wasn't recoiling from it any more. He felt like he was flying along on top of a cloud. At this rate he felt he could go anywhere.

'Hold on! Someone's fallen!' Doi called out.

It had to be Aizu. Noboru halted reluctantly and turned around. He could see huge amounts of powder swirling through the air, but this was very near him, and he remained in a totally white space.

'OK! You can carry on now!'

It was Yuko's voice this time. Noboru felt like she was talking to him alone, and he happily set off again. The wind shaved his cheeks like a sharp knife. He tightened the cords on his hood. He had to keep his field of vision clear, so periodically he scraped the snow off his goggles with his fingers.

Aizu fell down three more times. Once he must have fallen deep in fresh powder because it took some time to help him up.

Not long after they had got going again the wind

suddenly died, and, as if heavy white curtains were being raised, Noboru's field of vision dramatically improved. The snow was now falling straight down from the sky. The valley pressed in from both sides. He checked the compass again and saw they were heading west. As they had followed the left side of the valley so as not to miss the main branch of the Satsunai River, they had at some point passed the confluence of the Kinen Stream. Just as Yanagisawa had said they would.

Noboru halted and signalled that it was time for a break. He could now see back to where Yuko and Aizu were. Doi then appeared from out of the white.

'You OK?' Noboru asked, removing his goggles and gazing steadily at the snow-covered Yuko.

'Yes.' Yuko had taken off her goggles as well, and her eyelashes were covered with snow.

'We're not going to get stranded, but I haven't forgotten what you said back there,' Noboru said to her.

Yuko gave him a shy look and was silent. The dazzling smile of hers that had been in his mind had finally faded. A strong jolt was what had been needed, Noboru wanted to think, to do away with all the unseen difficulties that had been swirling around him.

Aizu, breathing hard, came up to them. His face was flushed.

'Any problems?' Noboru asked, giving the snow-covered Aizu a once-over.

'Sorry to slow everybody down.'

'Tomorrow we'll be climbing up the ridge so you won't have to ski. At most I'll have you take the lead and clear a path through the snow.'

'That'd be great.'

'Once we finish this trip you'll be a veteran mountain skier,' Noboru said, helping Aizu take off his backpack.

On the ground, the pack sank halfway into the snow. Mountains rose up sharply on both sides, and the valley was one big snowdrift. Noboru took off his own backpack then removed his skis, which he strapped to the backpack. Yuko gave him a sweet, and he popped it into his mouth. Doi set his backpack down, too, sitting down on it. Ariga and Yanagisawa appeared; both had smiles on their faces.

'I was sure the wind wouldn't last for ever, but for a while there I was wondering if we'd make it,' Yanagisawa said cheerfully to Noboru.

Noboru was considering whether this was the right time to reveal to Yuko how he felt about her.

Attached by the climbing rope, Yanagisawa and Ariga sat down on their packs. The wind creaked above them.

Aizu removed his woollen cap, and steam immediately rose from his head and was carried away by the wind.

'Aizu, glad to see you and the Hidaka Range are such good friends now – the way you were hugging each other all the time,' Yanagisawa said.

'I'm worn out,' Aizu laughed, running his fingers through his hair, which was already frozen.

'You can't be worn out just yet. You still have to dig a snow cave,' Ariga said, his tone unexpectedly serious.

As he gazed down at the map, Noboru wiggled his toes inside his boots, trying to get the circulation going. 'Shall we go to the confluence of the Junosawa?'

'Shouldn't be a problem.'

'Like we planned.'

'We're lucky to be on schedule after a blizzard like that.'

'We're on track.'

This last exchange was between Yanagisawa and Ariga. One learned a lot in the mountains. No matter how foul the weather might be the situation changes from moment to moment, and bad conditions don't last for ever. If you can somehow hold on, things will always get better.

'Gotta take a leak,' Aizu said and stood up. He took three steps downwind when his right leg sank up to his groin in snow. He righted himself, and now his left leg sank as well. It was a snowdrift, and there had to be at least of three metres of accumulation – soft fresh powder at that.

'Just do it right there. We'll watch you,' Yanagisawa said, laughing.

'Yeah, anywhere's fine,' Ariga joined in.

Aizu struggled to get out from the drift, but the harder he tried the deeper he sank. Noboru, tamping down the snow as he approached Aizu, held out a ski pole to him. Like someone drowning, Aizu clung to it. Noboru yanked hard, which caused his own right foot to sink into the snow. Everyone laughed. Who should come to Noboru's rescue but Yuko. She grabbed on to his free hand and pulled for all she was worth. Aizu held on to the pole and eventually managed to crawl out of the deep drift. Noboru, Yuko and Aizu sprawled out on the snow while the other three continued to laugh.

The sky looked ready to dump some more snow. In fact, the sky and the snow were indistinguishable. The mountains in winter were a world of death, but his being in them like this made Noboru feel keenly alive. Heart pounding, he could feel blood pulsing through his body. When I breathe deeply my blood is filled with oxygen. *I'm alive!* Noboru thought as he held on to Yuko's hand.

The Satsunai River ran west, but they gradually changed back from a north-northwest direction to northwest. The wind should pick up but wouldn't be as strong as before. The seniors took turns to lead, and they wisely chose the route where the wind was weakest. If it had been summer they would be clambering over boulders piled on boulders and water flowing between them, and occasionally they would get wet up to their waists and then have to plough through thick undergrowth. But now everything was buried in snow, making a single beautiful path. Some wind might blow, but it would be embarrassing to call this a hardship.

In the shadow of a huge rock stood a tree that looked like a jewel – it was an ice-encased dakekanba. In the wind its branches scraped against one another with a faint clatter. With its flowers covered in ice, the tree looked like something that should be in heaven not on earth. The six members of the group just stood and gazed at it. If the snow would stop and sunlight pour down on it, it would be even more beautiful, Noboru thought. He exchanged a glance with Yuko, who seemed happy to have shared a moment such as this. This first dakekanba led to a line of similar trees, as if the whole forest were filled with them.

The wind let up but not the snow. Before they realized it, the thick clouds had drifted away and the sky was covered by thin clouds that seemed translucent, like frosted glass.

From these clouds snowflakes fluttered to earth. It was a gorgeous scene, but Noboru knew the dangers. Hexagonal snowflakes were falling unbroken, their shapes intact. Because there was no wind they weren't hitting each other, so the crystals that formed the flakes were building up in parallel, only touching at their edges, and not piling up on top of each other and making for a stronger structure. This would lead to a weak layer of snow – a condition ripe for an avalanche.

The snow on the mountains began to look like layers of hexagonal snow crystals – like countless knives piled up on each other, their edges sharp and menacing. Noboru thought about this as he moved on, while the cloud cover grew thicker and the wind picked up again. This would cause the snow crystals to break up and create more compacted snow. But since the weak layer wouldn't break up there would still be a danger of a surface avalanche. With this snow and wind overhangs would develop, too.

Before 2 p.m. they arrived at the confluence of the Junosawa. The valley had grown narrower the deeper they went into the mountains. If they encountered white-out conditions here they would be stuck, but fortunately visibility was good. The mountains around them were steep, and if there were an avalanche it would most likely head towards this valley. They had to get out of the valley as quickly as they could, but they would have to camp here at least one night. Early the next morning they would climb to the ridge on the left bank of the Junosawa, and on the edge of the valley they would camp on the ridge connecting Esaomantottabetsu and Kamuiekuuchikaushi.

It was narrow, but a stream was always a great path for mountain skiing. If it were only downhill it would be wonderful. They had undone the rope long before, but the line of climbers was staying together. Aizu's skiing was improving by the minute. Anyone who goes up into the mountains learns a lot. Noboru himself hadn't been taught to ski by anyone but through similar experience. You keep on falling, and your body learns what to do. Whatever you learn in the mountains your body does not forget.

'Why don't we dig a snow hole?' Yanagisawa suggested with a smile. 'It's more comfortable than a tent.' Yanagisawa's smile never faded, not here in the mountains nor back in town. The harder things were, the brighter he smiled.

'If we want to be safe from avalanches, we'd better go up pretty high,' Ariga said, looking up at the slopes of the mountain, cautious as always.

Here, again, the presence of Yanagisawa and Ariga led to a decision in critical situations, without them really discussing it. Noboru's own opinion usually stood somewhere in between, and he would listen to both before making a decision. And this was always accepted as the final word.

All vegetation was buried deep beneath the snow, and only the largest trees were visible. But the slope was steep. They would climb up this slope and dig a snow hole. They would come down tomorrow morning and follow the stream bed until they reached the ridge. Their lives were on the line, and they couldn't cut corners.

'Skis are useless from here, so let's change into snowshoes,' Noboru called out to the group.

'Bet that makes you happy, Aizu,' Yanagisawa added, provoking some laugher.

'I wanted to practise my skiing a little more. I'm just getting into the swing of it,' Aizu replied. Everyone laughed at that, too.

It was still snowing hard. The wind caused it to swirl up from the ground, slam into trees and break into bits, then reform and crawl up the slope.

The climbers got their snowshoes out and tied their skis to the side straps of their backpacks, one on each side, and tied the tips together with a belt.

'Aizu likes skiing, and I like Yuko,' Yanagisawa said, almost singing.

Everyone looked at him in surprise, including – Noboru was sure – Yuko, although he couldn't see her expression. Restraining himself, he avoided looking at Yanagisawa. He could feel, painfully, how tense the mood had suddenly become.

'Oh, did I say something out loud?' Yanagisawa said, pretending to ask the nearby Ariga.

'You said something about liking skiing,' Ariga answered.

'I like all my climbing friends,' said Yanagisawa, dodging the subject and directing his words at Noboru.

Perhaps Yanagisawa had detected the feelings growing between Noboru and Yuko. But Noboru didn't care, as he felt that he and Yuko had already reached an understanding. Noboru rose up and stamped his feet to make sure his snowshoes were securely fastened. The snow was quite soft, and it was going to be hard work to blaze a trail through the snow.

'Yanagisawa, you're in fine form. Why don't you take the lead,' Noboru said, wanting to challenge him.

'This is going to be tough. Let's start by leaving our backpacks and making a path. If we try this with our packs on we'll run out of steam. It'll need two people,' Yanagisawa said, staring at Noboru.

Noboru had no choice but to reply, 'Sounds good. You and I will make the path, and while we're doing that we'll look for a place to dig a snow hole.'

They both knew just how backbreaking a task it was to plough a way through the deep snow. Noboru, as leader, went first. The snow was up to his chest, and, to make things worse, the slope was steep. The snow was powdery, and it was like breaking through a wall. Noboru hit his knees twice, three times against this wall, stepped on to the collapsed snow, gathering it up with his hands and compacting it, then trampling it all down with his snowshoes. This made up one step. As he put his weight down, the snow under him made a creaking sound. Halfway down he stopped sinking. That was another step, and it had left Noboru sweaty, his shoulders heaving as he gulped air. He repeated the same actions with his left foot. What was needed was strength and endurance. The todomatsu pines, coated with snow, looked like a line of enemy soldiers just waiting for Noboru and the group. Noboru struggled and managed another step forward. His breathing was so laboured it felt like his lungs would burst. He turned around and saw Yuko looking at him from close by. He had only moved two metres.

'Time to swap,' Yanagisawa said, and Noboru got out of the way. Using a shovel, Yanagisawa dug into the snow, chucking it on either side to make a path. The shovel could only make a space wide enough to put your feet, and you still had the trying task of ploughing through. After two metres Yanagisawa collapsed on top of the snow, his face flushed, his chest heaving. Noboru picked up the shovel and started to dig.

The forest was a mix of conifers and deciduous trees. The todomatsu and ezo matsu now seemed a bit more like ascetics practising meditation, while the leafless trees slumbered, their nakedness exposed. When Noboru took a breather, a profound silence filled the air. Within this silence he could feel the trees asleep. Everything was asleep except for the noisy humans.

Ariga and the younger members got in on the act, helping to create a trail through the snow. Until they got to the ridgeline of the Junosawa, that's what they would have to do. Even if they had to switch every two metres, with six people they should be able to make some progress. Once you made a foothold you didn't immediately step forwards. You pulled your foot backwards, rested a beat, then stepped forwards. This allowed the snow crystals to adhere to each other and better support your weight. Without destroying these sharp, delicate crystals, you couldn't take a single step.

It was Noboru's turn again to do battle with the snow. He couldn't help but feel how powerless his body was – the bones, tendons, flesh and blood – in the face of the snow, which was the inexhaustible power of the mountains. He used the shovel and took a step forwards, made sure the snow could hold him and shifted his weight on to it. That was all he could do. From what he could see of the trees, he estimated an accumulation of over three metres of snow. If he stepped where the snow crystals had not frozen, he might sink into the soft snow and drown. A sea of snow. And as they struggled forward snow kept on falling. The passion of the mountains never let up.

But what was the point of all this power and passion? The air that crosses over from the Sea of Japan, warm and heavy with moisture, creates a convection phenomenon in which the warm air goes up higher and the cooler air descends, releasing cold moisture into the upper atmosphere. This is what caused such massive amounts of snow to fall, but to Noboru it felt as if the mountains were rejecting human beings. This was the land of Kanna Kamui, after all.

The plan for the group, after they made their way along the ridge, was to climb Mount Poroshiri in five days' time. When a snowstorm hit the mountains, and human beings couldn't enter the area, the gods played along the peaks of the Hidaka. While he mulled this over, Noboru made it two metres further, and then, his breathing laboured, retreated and crouched in silence. When he had caught his breath, he looked up and saw that Yuko was now battling the wall of snow. She seemed about to be blown back at any moment, but she kept going for all she was worth.

There was no guarantee that they would be safe if they could get to a certain height. The higher they climbed from the stream, the further they would be from danger, but they would then need to dig a snow hole. When they were not trying to make a trail through the snow they hauled their backpacks along. The strong wind died down, but the snow did not stop. They couldn't see the whole valley, but it was clear that they had climbed fairly high up. Although not confident that they were out of the range of an avalanche, Noboru told the group that they ought to be fine where they were. The gentle slope had yielded to a sudden steep incline that towered above them. This would make digging a snow hole easier, and there would be plenty of snow for a roof, so the shelter should be strong enough. And now they had a path back down to the river, too.

There was a popping sound, like sparks going off. Noboru glanced around. The frozen branches of trees were snapping against each other in the wind. Perhaps this was how the lonely, slumbering trees established that there were other trees near by. With their tough bark they seemed to be wearing tight-fitting coats. If they stood there long enough, eventually the snow would melt and leaf buds would swell. When they burst open, light green leaves would appear, becoming darker as the sunlight grew stronger. Rain would fall and soak into the soil, and the tree roots would thirstily absorb the moisture. And before you knew it the trees would have grown taller. Roots would spread out, trunks would thicken, and the treetops would steadily push towards the sky. At some point, the green would start to fade from the leaves, and the whole tree would grow dry. The leaves on the branches would flutter away, one by one, with nothing to stop them. The tree was oblivious, but all around it the world was changing.

'Let's dig the snow hole right here,' Noboru announced. Taking the shovel from Doi he began to carve out where the entrance would be.

'Let's dig from both sides. Later we can fill in one side,'

said Yanagisawa, drawing a square on the slope with a saw, which he then passed to Aizu, who began to cut through the snow, taking large blocks.

Noboru dug for a while, then handed the shovel to Doi. Since there were snowdrifts from the wooded valley side, not much wind would blow into the entrance. They created a small terrace in front of it. Noboru felt reassured, once again, that this was a satisfactory spot for a snow hole.

Doi dug in quite deep, and something like a corridor began to take shape. Yuko spread out a tent to collect the dug-out snow. When there was a pile of it she pulled it outside. Noboru stepped over to help her. When they got it to the slope, they rolled the snow off and down. Yuko was smiling as she did this, and Noboru felt he had to say something.

'Does your sixth sense tell you we're still going to get stranded?'

Noboru knew how this mountain frightened Yuko. The fact that she didn't try to hide her fear made Noboru feel even more tender towards her. No matter how much experience an alpinist had, no, actually the more experience an alpinist had, the more frightening winter mountains seemed. But no matter, he told himself – he was the group leader and he had to make sure their lives were safe.

'Sorry, it was a stupid thing to say,' Yuko said.

'Anybody would be afraid in a snowstorm like that.'

'Even you?'

'Absolutely. In the mountains you learn how weak human beings are. But that's OK. I always feel vulnerable in the mountains. And because you're vulnerable, you feel afraid. You have to use your knowledge and experience, or you won't survive. We struggle like this, and what we end up learning is how weak we really are. And the scenery's beautiful, too.'

From the strong-willed person Noboru had seen in the snowstorm Yuko was back to being an ordinary girl, and this made Noboru feel that she was his again. He put his arm around her shoulder and drew her close, and as if she had been waiting for this she clung to him.

'I climbed the mountains last winter so I thought I'd be much stronger. But I'm scared of everything,' she said into his chest, on the verge of tears.

Her honesty made Noboru happy. Yuko's fears were probably shared by the majority of their party, and Noboru was not unsympathetic, but he knew that once they were about halfway through their itinerary unease would turn to joy. The deeper the initial fear, the stronger the eventual joy. But this fear was something you had to overcome on your own.

'Just trust me,' he said.

'OK.'

Noboru could tell that her smile was forced. She looked as if she were about to cry, and he wondered if he had alarmed her more than he had reassured her.

'Sleep next to me tonight. Don't worry – I won't try anything.'

Yuko clung to him tighter, and even through the thick clothing Noboru could feel the warmth of her body. I love you, he whispered silently.

'You don't mind?' she asked. Her upturned face was a mix of unease and gladness.

'Of course not. When you can't sleep you use up good energy. And that causes accidents.'

Yanagisawa and Ariga appeared as Noboru said this, pulling the other spread-out tent laden with snow. Noboru and Yuko quickly moved apart. Noboru started walking back to the group, urging her to do the same. As Noboru passed, Yanagisawa shot him a look that knifed through him.

Noboru began to shave the wall of snow with the cooking pot. Doi continued shovelling out a corridor, and Yuko followed his lead. As if pressed for time, Doi shovelled energetically, digging deeper and deeper. When the pile of snow at his feet got to a certain height, Noboru signalled to Yuko with his eyes and the two of them dragged the tent out to dispose of the snow.

In silence the group worked on, wanting to finish by nightfall.

Inside the hole, the snow sparkled light grey as the group began shovelling out a room. Noboru worked alongside Aizu, who was using the saw, and Yanagisawa, who was using an ice axe. When the tent spread out in the corridor was full, Noboru pulled it out of the way to dump its contents. The falling snow wasn't letting up, softly accumulating on the snow they had shifted.

Yuko's complexion seemed less pale, probably because she had been active. 'Are you feeling any better?' he asked. Noboru himself felt relieved enough to talk with her again.

'Yes, I am,' she said, her eyes smiling.

Yuko, who looked too delicate to climb mountains, was a beautiful woman. To Noboru, she looked more attractive here in the mountains than back in the city.

'Once we're inside the snow hole it'll be just like being at home. Doesn't matter how hard it snows or blows outside. And when we light a fire it'll be warm.'

'Good.'

'In the summer why don't we cross the Hidaka together – just the two of us? We'll smell the leaves and laugh about what it was like back in the snow hole. And talk about our future.' Noboru was able to say this without becoming too nervous.

'OK!' Yuko replied, her smile deeper than before.

Noboru wanted to hold her to him but restrained himself. Things were decided between them now, so there was no need to rush. If he made his feelings for her any more obvious the group would fall apart.

'If we hike in summer, we can be by ourselves,' Noboru said in a low voice, which caused Yuko to blush and look down smiling. As Noboru took the lead dragging the tent, he wanted to run for joy. The falling snow appeared to him like flowers in full bloom. If the snowflakes were flowers, there would be countless flowers. And if they were flowers, they had to be beautiful.

As soon as he re-entered the snow hole, which was slightly darker than outside, Noboru put on a studied, bored expression. The other four members of the group were on their knees, scraping and digging. The height of the hole was calculated so that there would be air space of fifty centimetres between the ceiling and their heads when sitting cross-legged on the floor; otherwise claustrophobia might result. Noboru scraped the ceiling to create a dome, so that in the event of the snow inside the hole beginning to melt the water wouldn't drip on them but would follow the curve of the dome and roll down the wall instead.

On the ground sleeping space was two metres by fifty centimetres for each person. These measurements, multiplied by six – with a little extra for the people sleeping on the edges, so that they wouldn't be right up against the snow – gave the dimensions of the snow hole's interior.

They had started to sweat as they dug, so they removed the outer layer of their snowsuits. Once preparations for the snow hole were completed the only sound was their breathing. They spread out a tent on which to sit down and hung the second tent at the entrance as a door. They went outside, stuck their skis and poles in one spot, so they protruded from the snow, then stuck the shovel and axes in the snow to indicate the entrance to their snow hole. All they needed to do now was unpack, prepare the gas stove and food and lay out their sleeping-bags: then their new home in the snow would be complete. As they did this it grew dark. They lit a candle, and its light reflected brightly off the white ceiling and walls.

For dinner Yuko was making curry and rice. She had precut and parboiled potatoes, onions and carrots and put them in plastic bags. The vegetables had frozen naturally. In another bag was precooked pork, and it was frozen as well. One good thing about the mountains in winter was that you could bring fresh food with you. On the stove Yuko melted snow and heated the water, put in the vegetables and once they were warmed through, added the curry mix. The rice came in a retort pouch, which she heated up in a separate pot. While heating up the rice she added another pouch of small hamburger steaks into the curry.

'This is great!' Noboru couldn't help commenting as he brought a spoonful of curry to his mouth.

Yuko had boiled water for tea. She handed Noboru his mug, into which he poured a shot of whisky. The whisky canteen was passed around, and everyone did the same.

'We're really lucky to have such a great snow hole. No worries now,' Yanagisawa said in high spirits. 'When we were in the white-out and couldn't move I thought for sure we'd have to bivouac with our tents. Dig shallow one-man snow holes on the slope in the shade of the rocks and put the tent up over the entrance.'

Holding his mug in both hands Ariga stared down at the rising steam.

Despite himself, Noboru had also pictured them in that situation: sleeping-bag up to your chin, the wind howling so fiercely you couldn't sleep. You might fall asleep for while, but you'd wake up right away because of the cold. And you're afraid to fall asleep, thinking you'll never wake up again, but you're sucked up into this fear and fall asleep, only to awake up again. You're assaulted by an overpowering fear that you'll never escape from the pitch-black darkness around you. The night never ending.

'Do you know of any small jobs I could do? I had to quit my part-time job in order to come to the mountains,' Aizu said all of a sudden.

Ariga looked up from the hot water in his mug. 'I have to find a part-time job myself,' he said.

'Didn't you land a full-time job at a TV station?'

'Yeah, but –'

'I thought you were starting work a week after we come down from the mountains, right?'

'I poured all my money into the mountains, so I either have to get a part-time job for a couple of days or borrow money from somebody. How about you, Aizu? Can you lend me some cash? Anything will do,' Ariga joked.

Smiling broadly, Aizu replied, 'I'm the one who needs to borrow cash.'

'I won't run away, so your money's safe. I'll definitely pay you back.'

'I don't have a yen to spare. So there's nothing to lend.'

'If you're that strapped I'll lend you some,' Yuko said, jumping in.

'It's too risky. If you lend money to a beggar like him he'll make up some excuse not to pay you back,' Yanagisawa said, pouring a drop of whisky into his mug.

'It's all right,' Yuko said, somewhat peeved. 'I'm getting a scholarship. I'm not scrimping, just living normally, and this is money that's left over.'

Noboru listened contentedly to the conversation and imagined hiking with Yuko, just the two of them, in the summer. There wouldn't be any need, like now, to use the ridge to the left of the Junosawa and come out on to the brow of the mountain to make base camp there and climb Kamuiekuuchikaushi. Instead, they could climb up Stream No. 8 and reach the summit of Kamuiekuuchikaushi, then follow the ridgeline to reach the summits of Esaomantotta-betsu, Kamui, Totsutabetsu and Poroshiri. They wouldn't have to worry about avalanches, and so long as they didn't slip and fall it would be an enjoyable climb. And at night Yuko and he would be alone in their tent.

'How about we do it like this?' Yanagisawa said loudly, clapping his hands. 'I'll borrow cash from Yuko at no interest, then lend to all of you with interest?' Yanagisawa had a job with the Hokkaido prefectural government waiting for him.

'That's pretty shameless,' Noboru said, laughing. After graduation he, too, would be starting a job at a manufacturer of agricultural products. Like Yanagisawa, he had his entrance ceremony for new employees on 1 April. One week after they came down from the mountains he would have to get everything settled so he could begin his new life, like an entirely new person. Students who had graduated ahead of him had done the same thing, but he wondered whether he really could make such a major transition in such a short time.

'You should all come to my apartment, and I'll make you dinner,' Yuko said. 'I'll show you how good a cook I am.'

The first to react was Yanagisawa. 'That'd be fantastic,' he said.

So the group decided that after their climbing trip all would gather at Yuko's. Noboru was wishing he had been the only one invited, but of course he didn't say this. For a while, the group chatted about inconsequential things. Noboru was physically there but didn't participate in the conversation, his mind elsewhere.

Last summer, saying that he wanted to learn more about the Hidaka Range, Noboru had visited a dairy farm at the foot of the Hidaka run by a former member of the college climbing club. This was Mr Akasaka, the man who had driven them in his truck from Obihiro to the start of the trailhead at the Satsunai River. Akasaka had known about Noboru, a young member of his former club, had been pleased by his visit and had put him up at his house. For his part, Noboru had been hoping to meet him while he was in college. Akasaka – a quiet, unaffected man – was married to a classmate in the Agriculture Department, and the couple's daughter was just about to enter elementary school. After Noboru helped Akasaka with the evening milking and feeding of the cows he sat down to a home-cooked dinner and *shochu* liquor. As they ate Akasaka solemnly told him a story that Noboru now thought to share with the group in the snow hole, almost as if he were Akasaka telling the story himself.

'When a person dies in the mountains,' he began, 'his body is destroyed, but his soul lives on. Depending on the feelings of the survivors of the deceased, the soul either shines brightly or is forgotten.

'Mount Xuemen, approximately 400 kilometres west of Chengdu in Sichuan Province in China, is on the eastern edge of the Tibetan Plain and, rising to 7,643 metres, is the highest peak in the area. There aren't any sherpas as there are in Nepal, so our party had to divide up our gear and transport it ourselves over several trips. Porters helped carry our things to base camp, but from Camp 2 to Camp 5 at 6,900 metres, we had to carry everything by ourselves. From Camp 5 we made our assault on the summit. Many in the party complained of altitude sickness and headaches. But after painkillers, tranquillizers and anti-frostbite medicine all twelve of us reported feeling well. It had been a struggle just to get to where we were.

'This was the fifty-third day after we had left Japan, and thirty-seven days after the main group had set up base camp. Camp 5 was established in a saddle between two peaks. We walked along a snowfield for a while and hit a forty-degree wall of snow. We had to use our ice axes to scale it. It was snowing continuously; occasionally the sky was visible, but then the clouds would blow in again. Unsettled weather, but it could have been improving. Since we were in China we couldn't get a weather map, and we didn't know how the pressure systems were. Probably because of a steady north wind there were several snow overhangs on the south wall – if we'd stepped through them we'd have fallen or caused an avalanche. We climbed up the steep slope, where there was not such an accumulation of snow. Finally the clouds broke and we could see the summit of Mount Xuemen. It looked like a pure-white heavenly realm. The entire glacier was covered by a sea of clouds.

'The snow was compacted and only went up to the top of my boots, so the crampons held firm. But the air felt like it was being twisted out of you when you breathed, from the bottom of your lungs. No matter how deeply you breathed, it was rough going. We'd take a break, have a bite, but then could only go on five more steps. The snow at our feet was sometimes shallow, sometimes deep. The mist covering the glacier blew up the slope and immediately covered the summit. The fog became thicker and snow began to fall, the weather steadily getting worse. It was frustrating that my body would not respond. There were eight climbers ahead of me, and they faded in and out of view. We had different levels of stamina and conditioning, so we hadn't tied ourselves together with a climbing rope. The snow fell harder, and the wind picked up. I couldn't see the summit, and with no idea where I was I felt like I was suffering. I finally made it over a steep snow wall. As I was climbing up this slope, which was at an incline of least forty degrees, I thought how we would need a climbing rope on the way back. But I had no idea who had the rope or whether it'd been used for other purposes. I kept on climbing, listening to the sound of my heart. The only thing I knew I could count on was my sheer will to keep going, one step at a time. If I could keep on going I'd arrive at the most beautiful spot in the whole world. Because of the fog I was in a totally white world.

'I heard a sound like a bell, the sound rapidly descending from the sky. After a pause, I heard someone yell that one of the party had fallen. That meant certain death, but at the moment it didn't strike me that way. The word "fallen" reached me and then was gone. The mist let up a little, and I saw seven climbers ahead of me, descending the slope backwards. When I could see about fifty metres in front of me I made out a sharp cliff that looked like it had been chopped out with a hatchet. All I knew was that someone had been sucked down off that cliff. I tried sticking my ice axe into the snow. The snow was soft, and the axe disappeared. Even if you managed to get a purchase with your axe, it was a toss-up whether it would hold you. We had only one rope, forty metres long, and one of the party was using it to search for the missing climber. He was never found. I was fifty metres below and looked to our leader to see whether we should continue climbing or stand by. I checked the altimeter: it read 7,550 metres. The summit was only a hundred metres higher. It was so cold, standing on such a steep slope at such an altitude. I couldn't bear it. I thought about the climber who had fallen, and a feeling of dread came over me. I was shivering so hard I couldn't stand still. I never imagined I was this spineless. The seven climbers were slowly descending above me, all linked now to one climbing rope, seeming quite shaken by the incident. They were about fifty metres from where I was. I wanted to climb up to join them. I thought if I were left by myself I would slip and fall. Climbing up, I was so absorbed in reaching the summit, but now I was a lump of solid fear. I could see the first climber now descending. He was sticking his axe in the snow, the rope secured around his waist. He crouched down on the snow and the climber at the other end did the same, forming a fulcrum down which the five other climbers could descend. I knew what they were feeling – a mixture of fear, after seeing one of your own fall to his death, and the kind of brain freeze that comes from altitude sickness. But I didn't feel this was a dangerous situation. And I expected the others felt the same. Because they were all seven attached, each by his own carabiner, to a single climbing rope. All seven of them got to about five metres from where I was. Suddenly, one of them slipped and slid down the slope, pulling the rope taut. The two climbers on either side, who should have kept him from falling further, found their feet pulled out from under them at the same instant, and fell. The weight of these three pulled down the two adjacent climbers. The guy closest to me looked at me, sheer panic in his face, but he couldn't say anything. The rope pulled taut, the pressure tugging at his carabiner, and he was dragged down, as if slapping against the snow. His movements seemed to take place in slow motion.

'It was strange that not a single one of them tried to break their descent by digging into the snow with their ice axe. It was like they knew this was their fate and there was no fighting it. Some of them had their faces to the snow, others their backs to it, and silently, incredibly fast, they sped down the slope. And then they were gone, disappeared, just like that. Even now sometimes I can see it all happening to them, clear as day.'

Akasaka sobbed as he finished his tale. Reports of this accident, which had taken eight lives, had been in the newspapers and were quite well known, but Noboru now had heard the account directly from Akasaka, who – no doubt driven by some need – had obviously spoken from the depths of his heart.

'The souls of other people live on in us. Those eight people live in me, and often they help me around the dairy. So I'm always talking with them. I've never forgotten them.' Akasaka was silent now as he sipped more *shochu*.

'Darling,' his wife said, her tone gentle, 'I think you've had enough. You always get like this when you've been drinking.'

'Just don't die in the mountains. Too much sorrow for those left behind,' Akasaka said, as he stumbled to his feet and went off to bed.

Akasaka's wife showed Noboru where he was to sleep. A futon, fragrant with sunshine and grass, was spread out for him, and he thanked her profusely. Noboru wasn't usually this voluble, and he knew he himself was drunk. He hadn't witnessed the faces of the seven climbers as they silently tumbled down the steep snowy slope, but he could see them vividly in his mind. He wondered how terrifying it must have been to be dragged by all the weight, down into the abyss of death – until you slammed into blocks of ice and rocks and lost consciousness for ever.

'Unless you come down alive, I don't call that mountain climbing. It's OK for the person who dies because his soul remains in the mountain, but it's awful for the people left behind. Mountain climbing shouldn't be about creating sadness. It should create joy.' Noboru repeated these words of Akasaka's aloud. Mountains are certainly dangerous places. There are snares, everywhere, leading to death. Slipping past these snares, and making it back alive – there's the appeal. Mountains in winter especially are a world of death. Sometimes you lose the fear of death. You know that if you don't do anything, you will most definitely perish. Dying isn't all that hard.

'I'm not thinking about dying at all. Because after we get home Yuko's going to make us dinner at her place. Noboru, you bring three kilos of beef, the best quality you can find. I'll bring shirataki noodles and leeks. We'll have a fantastic sukiyaki,' Yanagisawa said in a very upbeat tone, almost singing.

Although Noboru was in the same snow hole as the others, he realized he had been off in a different world. He couldn't remember how far he had gone in relating Akasaka's story. The walls of the snow hole sparkled in the candlelight, like crushed gems. Everything looked beautiful to Noboru. Yuko's face, lit by the candle, had a gorgeous smile that was light itself. This place is far away from death, he thought.

Still smiling, Yuko began to speak. 'I'll do the cooking. You don't have to bring anything.'

'Well, be that as it may, these guys can eat, so you'd better be sure you make enough,' Yanagisawa said, laughing.

Hoping to be rejoin this harmless conversation, Noboru said, 'I'll be getting a salary, so I should be able to afford three kilos of beef. We can celebrate the graduation of the three final-year students while we're at it.'

'If we're celebrating that, then we can't have them bringing the meat, can we?' Yuko replied, her face sunny.

One day that smile might be all mine, Noboru thought happily. 'They can really pack it away, so I'll get cheap meat. It's no problem at all. Quantity's more important than quality here. Can't have you picking up the whole bill.'

A snow hole was the best thing when camping in the mountains in winter. They had the gas stove going, and the place was getting warm. Snow was good thermal insulation, and at the same time it let air pass through so they didn't need to worry about ventilation. If it got too hot the ceiling might start to sag, but if that happened all they needed to do was dig the floor out deeper. There might be a snowstorm, and they wouldn't hear a sound.

But if it did snow hard – as it was now – they would have to shovel the snow from the entrance, to keep it unobstructed.

Aizu brought out his camera and took photos of the

group, the flashes bouncing off the walls. Noboru smiled for the first few photos, but then stopped, his mind on other things. He felt so snug in the snow hole he could almost forget the heavy snow that was keeping them in. An avalanche was the thing to fear, but since they had built the snow hole high up the slope, away from the ridgeline of the main peak, they should be safe. If an avalanche did strike, though, their being inside the snow hole meant they couldn't get out of its way.

Ariga was listening to the radio. Suddenly he turned the volume up so everybody could hear the weather report. '. . . a severe cold front moving through that will bring the temperature in the upper atmosphere down to forty degrees below zero Celsius at an altitude of 6,000 metres.' Warm air containing a great deal of moisture was rising, releasing moisture into the cold air of the upper atmosphere. In short, the snow would continue for some time.

'We have food, so we'll just wait it out,' Yanagisawa said optimistically. 'Life in a snow hole isn't so bad.'

Even if they stayed put for two or three days they would still have to fight through the heavy snow both going and coming. They might have to start revising their plan, give up on climbing Poroshiri and use the snow hole as base camp to attack Kamuiekuuchikaushi. Or maybe they would have to evacuate . . .

'We should go to sleep pretty soon. We get up at 4 a.m. tomorrow. I'll see what the weather's like before I make any decisions. I'll get up once during the night and shovel off the snow. If anybody gets up to go to the toilet, remove a little of the snow if you can.'

Noboru said this in his best leader-like voice. With the bad weather there would be many more times when he would have to make decisions as the group leader. Aizu and Doi took the shovel and saw and cut out a shelf on the wall for the cooking gear, tableware and food. As Noboru smoothed out the floor and spread out a tent, he shot a glance at Yuko and, without worrying if anyone else noticed, motioned for her to come over to him.

'You should sleep in the middle,' Noboru said. 'Mountain men have to protect their women.' As Yuko stood beside him, no one else reacted, which only made Noboru more self-conscious.

With a movement that looked deliberate Yanagisawa tossed his gear down on the other side of Yuko. Of course Noboru couldn't say anything about this. On the other side of Yanagisawa would be Ariga. The two youngest students were to be at either end, where they could touch the wall. Silently, everyone blew up their mattresses and laid out their sleeping-bags inside the covers. Noboru was about to get inside his sleeping-bag wearing his rubber-soled inner boots but thought he should relieve himself first.

He pulled on his snowsuit and, bending over a little, passed through the corridor. The light from his head-torch hit the wall and curved away, and at the entrance was blocked by the curtain of falling snow. Each snowflake glistened as if on fire, dancing as if alive. Aizu had followed Noboru out. The snow around their snow hole was trampled down so they were on firm footing, but if they took a step away they would sink into deep powder.

They walked over to a spot about two metres from the

snow hole and urinated as they faced the mountain. The arc of Noboru's urine did not describe a neat parabola; it seemed to scatter as mist. Nor did it create a hole in the snow, smothered as it was by the falling snow. It was no different with Aizu's.

The cold penetrated Noboru's bones. 'This is great,' Noboru said, shivering as he zipped up.

'Great, yes, brilliant.'

'I think I'm going to go have some hot sake over at that bar. Have them grill me some squid, too.'

'It warms the body?'

'And the soul.'

Noboru shivered again, grabbed his arms together in front of his chest, bent over and went back into the snow hole. His cheeks immediately felt the warm, humid air.

'I wonder what the deer do when it snows like this,' Yanagisawa was saying.

'They go back to their home town,' Ariga replied.

'But it's snowing there as well.'

'Snow everywhere you go.'

As he listened to them, Noboru rolled up his snowsuit to use as a pillow. Wearing his inner shoes, he snuggled into his sleeping-bag, sticking his feet into his empty backpack. As Yuko exited the snow hole, the light from her head-torch wavering against the walls, Noboru opened up the map. It felt like snow was piling up on the map as well. He traced the Satsunai River upstream to the Junosawa confluence. With a mechanical pencil he noted the location of their present spot with 'March 13: Camp'. The ink in ballpoint pens froze in the mountains, so pencils were the writing implements of choice. When Yuko returned, snow on her hair and shoulders, he put the map back into its plastic case and placed it in front of his hiking boots near his pillow.

'Welcome back,' he said.

'Thanks,' she replied, brushing off the snow.

He thought Yuko said this, but he couldn't be sure. It could've been Yanagisawa, who seemed to be looking over at her. *Thanks,* Noboru tried mouthing the word to himself silently. He heard Yuko's breath as she blew out the candle, and then darkness descended. Yuko, walking near his head, stepped on the plastic map case, which made a crunch like when someone steps on a leaf. From behind, he could feel her bending over and sitting down on her sleeping-bag. And then Yuko, inner shoes first, slipped into her bag. Suddenly, Noboru could feel her breathing quite close to him. Yuko squirmed around in her sleeping-bag to get comfortable. He heard her zipping up.

'Good night.'

Yuko's voice, spoken to whom he wasn't sure, went straight into him and made him happy.

'G'night.'

Noboru was the only one who replied. Beyond Yuko he heard the rustle of a sleeping-bag. That had to be Yanagisawa. He could hear the wind blowing. It twisted and creaked, and he could sense the disturbance of the entire mountain. Their climbing itinerary was for a fourteen-day outing, including five rest days, and they had only just started. There was no reason whatsoever to be pessimistic, Noboru told himself. He opened his eyes and saw the wall of snow faintly gleaming. There was no light source, so the light had to be coming from within the snow. He wanted to get up and run his fingers over the wall, its bumps and depressions, but instead he lay still, not stirring. He slowly turned his face, trying to keep the snowsuit pillow from making a sound, and peered at Yuko's profile. She had the hood of her sleeping-bag up. A hint of light came to rest on the ridge of her nicely shaped nose. The hood moved slightly with each breath she took, but he couldn't tell if she was asleep yet or not. Before long Noboru was breathing in tandem with her.

He closed his eyes, enveloped in the afterimage of her face.

Being snowed in like this – wasn't it to be expected in the mountains in winter? Our climb, Noboru told himself, is going to be a success. He felt encased in warmth. The memory of skiing through the white-out came back to him, and exhaustion welled up from deep within.

He woke up, feeling as if he had floated to the surface from underwater. He quietly turned his head and saw Yuko, as before, only her nose visible. For a time, he gazed at her nose. He didn't really have to go to the bathroom, but he silently got himself out from the sleeping-bag and pulled on his climbing boots. He stood up and looked down at the sleeping Yuko. It was too dark to see her nose and mouth clearly. He pulled on his snowsuit and slipped on his gloves. The darkness was filled with the peaceful sounds of five people asleep.

Once outside he was met with a mound of snow. He reached for the shovel, which was covered in soft snow. The aluminium felt like a living thing. He thrust the shovel a few times into the mound, and it easily collapsed. Out in the darkness there was just snow. An infinite number of layers. You could never escape this world of snow. Noboru pulled the hood of his snowsuit over his head and tentatively took a few steps away. He removed his gloves and tried to urinate, but hardly anything came out.

He brushed the snow off the draped tent that was serving as a door, and went back inside the snow hole. The breathing of the five sleepers was disturbed, and he realized he had brought in cold air with him. Noboru gazed once more towards Yuko's face as he snuggled back into his sleeping-bag. Again, just having her beside him made him calm. He felt content and happy. He shut his eyes, knowing he would sleep soundly.

How much time had passed he wasn't sure, but somewhere between dream and reality he heard the distant sound of waves. He entertained the idea that they were waves lapping at the shore of the garden paradise at the summit of Mount Poroshiri, where Kanna Kamui played – and where sea lions are at their games, simple and innocent, unafraid of human hunters. A divine land beyond approach, even as Noboru and his group were heading there, drawing closer step by step. If they hadn't been stopped by the snow, they would have been in the land of the gods the day after tomorrow.

The sound of the waves grew quickly nearer and nearer. It became louder and stronger, and the ground began to rumble. By the time Noboru realized it was an avalanche he was surrounded by a deep thunder. Noboru was in the mouth of something that would swallow everything around it whole, and he was frozen in fear.

A large milk-filled udder dangled in front of him. Under the dry pink skin was a network of indigo-blue veins, like a map of train lines. The udder was warm to the touch, and he could feel the weight of it. Noboru followed Akasaka's instructions. He dipped a towel in disinfectant, wrung it out and wiped the light pink, almost translucent teat. The teat was not so fragile as it appeared to be. After disinfecting it he took the teat between his index and middle fingers, squeezed out some milk into a bucket and threw it out, because the first squeeze of milk contained bacteria. After cleaning all four teats, he manoeuvred them into the adhesive suction discs. The machine sucked like a calf would and then carried the foamy white milk away in clear plastic tubing along the ceiling. During milking times the barn became brighter.

'That's it. You've got it,' said Akasaka, standing in the next row. 'After you finish there, come over here.' The cows, their udders about to burst, half-closed their eyes in contentment as they were being milked. Next to them other cows were eating, urinating – whatever they felt like doing. When Noboru stood up he saw a row of cows, their backs lined up like so many ridges.

Mrs Akasaka had brought over a cart of hay and was using a pitchfork to feed the cows that had already been milked. They slowly lowered their heads and began munching. These mountain-sized creatures were chained together, using a ring through their nose, and couldn't go anywhere. When milk stopped flowing through the milking machine, that cow was done. Noboru then disinfected their teats once again as a guard against mastitis.

After Noboru had finished with his row of cows he went over to Akasaka. Several men – eight by Noboru's count – were gathered around, discussing the situation.

'I think you should try pulling it.'

'It's probably a breech birth.'

'You'd better get it out soon, or it'll suffocate.'

'No, just let nature take its course.'

'If we don't do anything the mother's going to suffer.'

'No, it's going to come out pretty soon.'

The men all had strong opinions and couldn't arrive at a consensus. From between the mother's hind legs Noboru could see two feet of the calf, up to the ankles. Each time the mother breathed, the ankles shook and then stuck out again. The cow's bloodshot eyes were full of tears. The cows next to her seemed oblivious to her suffering and went on placidly chewing their cud, clear drool dripping down the side of their mouths.

'If it takes too long both mother and calf will be unable to bear it. Let's pull it out,' said Akasaka. The decision made, everyone knew what they had to do. He brought over a thick rope and tied it around the calf's spindly ankles. The rope was not pristine, stained with blood and bodily fluids. Akasaka and the eight men grabbed hold of the rope. There was no room for Noboru, who thought that so many hands were too many anyway. While he stood and watched the nine men pulled hard on the rope, and the wet calf, like so much excreted matter, plopped out on to an old blanket laid out on the hay. Akasaka moved swiftly, untying the rope from its legs and stuffing hay into its nostrils to make it sneeze. That was the calf's very first breath.

Behind Akasaka the eight men gazed at the calf. 'It's a male,' one of the men announced.

'In a week you can sell it to be fattened for slaughter.'

'Ten days of life and that's it.'

'I guess we're luckier.'

Voices of different timbres echoed through the barn. Akasaka stood up and rested a hand on the mother cow's midsection.

'It's warm, so his legs won't fail him.'

This was Akasaka's way of saying that the birth had gone well. He went on, commenting to himself, 'Strange. If you overmilk them, or don't give them enough feed, they have male calves. I wonder why.'

The calf crouched with wide-open frightened eyes as if it didn't know where to look. Akasaka dragged the blanket with the calf still on it, skirting the row of cows, to place it in front of the mother. Seeing her offspring then for the first time she stuck out her whitish-pink tongue and gently licked the newborn, expelling the afterbirth at the same time.

Akasaka left the calf to be licked clean and set the placenta in front of the mother's mouth. She began devouring it noisily. The cows on either side of her showed no interest as they went on eating and defecating. Akasaka lifted the calf, which couldn't stand yet, and put it in a small enclosure by itself. Then he squeezed out the first milk for the calf from the mother, transferred it to a bucket with a rubber nipple on the bottom and fed the calf. The world is full of germs that, at any time, can take the life of the innocent; to counteract this the mother's milk contained antibodies that gave the calf immunity. After the calf had fed Akasaka stuck a couple of large calcium pills into the mother's mouth, rather as a kind of treat. Expressionless, the cow chewed the pills and swallowed.

Noboru suddenly became aware of the fact that the eight men had left. In the large fifty-head cow barn there were only Akasaka and his wife raking excrement into a gutter. As they silently worked on, the cows ignored them, flicking their tails to shoo flies away. Noboru knew he was watching this scene before him, but he was no longer a part of it. He was absent, and he found this absence strange. Neither Akasaka nor his wife noticed that he was missing from the scene, and Noboru couldn't fathom this.

He wasn't sure how long he had been walking. Luckily the snow wasn't deep, for if he had to plough his way through waist-deep snow he would have been exhausted long ago. Up ahead was a gentle peak that looked like a squashed sweet bun. In reality it was a sharp peak which couldn't maintain its shape because of the weight on it. To Noboru it looked like the breasts of an old woman lying on her back.

The road wasn't flat. When the road sloped down, the peak was no longer visible. It appeared again when the road rose, completely changed, the peak of the mountain pointing up, like youthful nipples. Noboru was worried that this was a different mountain, but the road had not branched off. He had just continued to walk down this one road and couldn't have gone astray.

The road twisted. The peak was now ahead of him, the road stretching towards it. If he followed the road he would reach the summit. He had been walking for such a long time, but the peak looked no closer. He felt that it was receding instead.

Still, all Noboru could do was trudge on, one step after another. He looked up at the peak, then down at his feet, and when he looked up again the peak had totally changed. Now it was flat again, as if it had been crushed, and the shape was slightly – no, completely – transformed.

He had come this far and couldn't very well turn back. Praying that the snow wouldn't get any deeper, that the road wouldn't vanish, Noboru walked on through this entirely white world. As he watched, the peak rose up, went slack, collapsed and rose up into another shape.

After he woke up he realized he had been dreaming. A faint low rumble, ominous from the start, was swiftly rushing towards them, snapping branches and devouring rocks as it swept forwards. Knowing that he was in a snow hole, wrapped inside his sleeping-bag, Noboru was helpless in the face of the approaching sound. Even if he stood up there was no place to run. He could sense Yuko and the others raising their heads. In an instant the gathering roar engulfed all the fear of this world, swallowing up everything in its path.

The fear trembled through his body, every hair on end. Noboru felt like he had been abandoned in an unknown darkness. The shock of being struck remained with him, like a flash of heat.

Not sure if this were a dream or real, Noboru sank deeper and deeper into the darkness. Along with a pressure that was crushing him . . .

Bathed in a green so fresh it was dripping, Noboru walked along lightly. The logging road was wide enough for Yuko and he to walk side by side. He wanted to show her that he was an older, experienced man. Pointing to a clump of bushes, Noboru said, 'Those are doronoki – balsam poplars. According to Ainu legend, they were the first things to grow on the earth. The *kamui* tried to rub branches of doronoki together to make fire – but without success. The next tree to appear was the elm; the *kamui* were able to make fire with it, and so the elm gained their respect. The cottonwood became jealous at this and turned into a *kamui* that brought on disasters. When there are epidemics evil spirits gather. You should never burn a cottonwood at this time because it will strengthen the evil spirits even more.'

Noboru had once tried to light a bonfire with some dry branches, not knowing they were from a cottonwood. They produced only smoke, and he had concluded this was an ungenerous tree.

As they walked down the gravel road, which was for logging trucks only and which led to a dead-end, Noboru thought what an unimpressive name doronoki was – literally, 'mud tree'. Through the green leaves of these mud trees he could hear the gurgle of the Satsunai River.

'But don't they use cottonwoods to make match splints?' Yuko asked after Noboru had finished, sounding as though she were refuting his point.

'Is that right?' Noboru replied in a muffled voice, his lips cold from the long-winded speech he had made. Since the wood didn't burn easily it made sense to use it for matches. Starting over, he said, 'Those trees are like us, I guess, with our unrefined muddy lives. We help other people but never get noticed for it.'

Once again he was assuming the stance of the older, more experienced person. He knew he was struggling to put a positive spin on his life, but hiking like this with Yuko – if this wasn't something positive, then what was?

'Elms are really nice trees, don't you think?' Yuko asked.

A large elm, looking as if it had gathered all the light of the surrounding greenery, stood beside their path, and Noboru and Yuko stopped to gaze up at the branches. A barely perceptible wind rustled the leaves, the greenish light filtering down like a shower. The light as it struck their faces had a tangible texture. Compared to the lives of humans, trees seemed to live for ever – although most didn't live to become massive like this. How many must have been cut down to make this logging road? This giant had barely escaped that fate.

Yuko approached the elm and pushed against the trunk with her hands. 'Humans first learned to use fire when lightning struck an elm,' she said.

In this forest, where eternity hung over everything, the

time that should have flowed over them slipped away between the trees, far ahead. Noboru looked back to see if anyone else was on the logging road.

'You can make a fire easily by rubbing an elm,' Yuko continued. 'I wonder who first discovered that? If you put some in a stove you can keep warm, like your grandmother holding you close.'

Noboru approached her from behind, circled around in front and kissed her lips, which were still moving as she spoke. Yuko gulped down the rest of what she was going to say as his tongue went deep into her mouth. The leaves rustled, the shower of light wavered. Noboru cupped Yuko's breasts through her shirt. A single touch told him everything he had needed to know. He could feel her heartbeat. Standing on her tiptoes, Yuko entwined her tongue around his, wholeheartedly and passionately. They were so close their eyelids touched, and a faint smile came to Noboru's face. Their tongues sought each other's, over and over.

They drew apart, connected by a strand of saliva that broke and vanished. Once apart, they were too shy to look each other in the eyes and instead looked down. They held hands and set off again. A construction site lay at the end of the logging road, a muddy minibus and backhoe in the lot. No one was around, and it wasn't clear what kind of construction was going on. They had taken a bus as far as they could, then walked the rest of the way. Noboru and Yuko, now lovers, wanted only to focus on one thing – themselves. At the river, they changed into boots for walking in the water.

There were no clear trails beyond this point. Noboru shouldered his pack with their tent, food and raingear. The weight bearing down on his ankles seemed heavier than before. He shifted the pack slightly side to side, testing its heft. He anticipated a thoroughly pleasant trip to the top of Kamuiekuuchikaushi, then back down.

At the end of the logging road there was a small box rather like a birdhouse. Noboru opened the lid, and on the laminated sheets of the notebook recording the names of hikers passing through he wrote his own name and address, adding 'with one companion'. He had planned on their spending two days' camping, but he had taken an extra day off as well, thinking they might go to a hot springs. These were the first paid holidays Noboru had taken since he started work.

They walked along, stepping on round rocks several times the size of a human head. Cottonwoods lined the banks. Between the dark green forest of cottonwoods and the white rocky streambed were the large leaves of the butterbur. Their river boots, lined with felt, gripped the rocks. There was less water in the river than usual, but they had to be careful where they would cross – they didn't want to slip and be pulled downstream with their heavy backpacks. Noboru walked right beside Yuko as they took one cautious step at a time through the water. As they got deeper into the river the unexpectedly strong current tugged at Yuko, and Noboru could feel her shaking a little nervously. Having crossed the river, they followed pink plastic ribbons tied to trees as signposts and entered the forest. They came to a slightly higher rise and then crossed the river once more.

Someone had left these ribbons as markers, and they were happy to trust that it was the best way to proceed. As they stood on each rock they leaned forwards, shifting the weight of the backpack forwards, and just as their centre of gravity shifted they leaped to the next rock. There were places where they had to leap on to two or three rocks in quick succession. Where it was dangerous they stepped into the water, choosing what seemed to be the shallowest spot. The water rose to their waist, and Noboru made sure to stay close to Yuko as they inched forwards. Even when the water was only up to their knees the current was strong enough to sweep them off their feet if they weren't careful. But the cold water felt good.

They entered the forest again, following the tattered pink markers. The wind had died out, leaving them hot and sweaty. Noboru felt that they were surrounded by new signs of life. He could hear birds. It was hard to tell which direction they were coming from, their calls echoing off the slopes. They reached the rocks and began their climb up and down, as water rushed by their feet. From between the trunks of the Yeddo spruce they saw something fly swiftly at the water, silver light sparkling like jewels on its choppy surface. The bird skimmed the surface and then vanished into the trees on the opposite shore.

'A crested kingfisher!' they exclaimed simultaneously. Noboru felt as if they were blessed. As long as he was with Yuko, the mountains, the sky – everything – was beautiful.

'How about taking a break?' Noboru asked.

'Sounds good.'

Noboru swung off his backpack. Compared to the

mountains in winter, there was little that weighed them down. Everything was pure delight. It was hard to believe this was the same spot they had been to in winter.

'I wonder what the other members of the climbing club are up to,' said Noboru.

Ken Yanagisawa worked at the Hokkaido prefectural office now, while Tadao Ariga worked at a television station. They lived near by, but Noboru had been so busy with his own job he hadn't seen them. As their lives took their own paths, perhaps their feelings were drifting apart. Or maybe they were just hesitating to come to see them, now that Noboru and Yuko were engaged to be married? Or perhaps they were a bit standoffish. He wanted to believe that if they were hiking together again, things would be like they used to be.

'Doi and Aizu should be climbing in the Taisetsu Range.'

'Time keeps flowing by,' Noboru said.

'That's for sure.'

'It's hard to keep things from changing.'

'They might seem to change, but they really haven't.'

'Maybe you're right.'

Noboru realized that what he had been saying was exactly what Yuko had been thinking. She had enriched his life more than he could say. As they sat there, side by side, he wrapped an arm around her, pulled her close and lightly kissed her. He knew they were alone, but still he reflexively glanced around to make sure Yanagisawa hadn't seen them. Several rays of silver light, like so many metal bars, shone through the deep green of the forest. Shining through the leaves, the light turned a slight green, too. Everything was absolutely beautiful. As they sat there together, silently gazing at the forest around them, Noboru stopped perspiring and felt a chill.

Each rock had burned white in the sun. Each time he stepped on one of the jutting rocks he nearly slipped. As Noboru made a little progress he would glance back, and Yuko was always right behind him. They exchanged glances. The small valley was a field of debris, a dangerous place if there were a heavy rain, for then there might be a flash flood. He couldn't see far ahead of him and couldn't make out the lay of the land. The ground between the rocks and boulders had been packed down by other feet and formed a kind of trail. The narrow trail sparkled whitely.

The same kind of field of debris met them at the top of the slope, but the white path went straight ahead to the bottom of the flat valley.

'How about buying a bird?' a voice suddenly said.

Noboru was completely startled. 'Yanagisawa! What're *you* doing here?'

'It doesn't matter what I'm doing here,' Yanagisawa answered curtly. He was squatting on top of a whitish rock, beside several small cages made of green bamboo. In each was a small bird. They weren't chirping, but they did seem to be breathing. 'How about buying a bird? Not for my sake but for yours. A hundred yen for one.'

'What am I supposed to do with it?' Noboru said, making sure that Yuko was right behind him. Deep down, he was feeling very disturbed.

'Well, you can let it go.'

Noboru didn't follow his meaning and remained silent.

Yanagisawa leaned forwards and explained, 'You let a captured bird fly free. I'm letting you do something really good. I'm sure you have a hundred yen on you.'

Noboru stuck his hand into a pocket and felt a cold coin there. He handed it over to Yanagisawa, and Yanagisawa passed him one of the homemade bamboo cages. The bird was trying to fly around, but the cage was too small and its wings kept flapping against the sides.

Yanagisawa had cut the bamboo himself, hand-woven the cages and caught the birds, which had gorgeous lazuline feathers. 'You have to build up a store of good works,' he said to Noboru, 'although it might be too late for that.'

Noboru pulled the string that opened the cage, and instantly the little bird flew off, its wings brushing Noboru's face. Reflexively Noboru shut his eyes, and he felt the breeze caused by the bird's wings on his eyelids.

When Noboru opened his eyes a second later the bird was already five metres away, flapping its wings furiously and flying into the vast azure sky. Could that be where the bird was meant to go? The bird flew steadily higher, disappearing into the sky as if melting into it.

'You did a good deed,' Yanagisawa said.

Noboru placed another hundred-yen coin on to his outstretched palm. Yanagisawa handed Noboru another bamboo cage. Noboru opened the cage and another lazuline-feathered bird flew soundlessly, except for the flap of its wings, into the sky. The sky seemed to be the little bird's plaything, and it easily hid itself.

‘Yuko, you should do a good deed, too. Especially if you’re going to be with this guy.’

Yuko gave Yanagisawa a hundred-yen coin and received a bamboo cage. The little bird sprung out of the greenish cage and disappeared into the sky. Noboru had any number of hundred-yen coins in his pocket, so he and Yuko continued to buy birds and to release them. It seemed as if the sky, bright to begin with, grew even brighter. They kept releasing the birds and still there was no end to them. Noboru enjoyed doing this with Yuko.

The five men were seated at a low table. It was the first time Noboru had met Yanagisawa, Ariga and Doi and Aizu, who were now in their second year, since March when the group of six had traversed Kamuiekuuchikaushi, Esaomantottabetsu and Poroshiri. They had planned on a leisurely expedition of nine days on the move and five days of rest, but a cold front had come in, producing an unusually heavy snowfall and obstructing their progress, and they used up all five of their off days and barely made it down by the scheduled time. The three seniors had graduated and begun their company jobs, and when they received their first pay cheques the group reunited at Yuko’s apartment for a meal, as they had promised in the snow hole. Noboru brought three kilos of beef, Yanagisawa brought the shirataki noodles and leeks, and Ariga brought the fried tofu and udon. Either Yanagisawa or Ariga brought the two large bottles of sake.

And as Yanagisawa rubbed the bottom of the sukiyaki

pot with a chunk of fat, he joked, 'I think the best thing to come out of our climb is that Aizu learned how to ski.'

'You can depend on me, when it comes to skiing,' Aizu laughed. 'Digging snow holes, too!'

'Make sure to put in lots of vegetables,' Ariga piped up.

The beef fat in the pot was melting, getting smaller as it slid around. Leeks were tossed into the sukiyaki pot, which had been borrowed from the mountaineering club, as had the two gas stoves they had taken climbing. Normally the beef would be added next, but then everyone would eat the beef before anything else. So the shungiku chrysanthemum greens, brought by one of the second-year students, were put into the pot. Noboru poured in sake, soy sauce and sugar from packets he had picked up at a coffee shop.

As they waited for the vegetables to cook Noboru said, 'Aizu, you were having so much trouble skiing I felt sorry for you, but it was amazing how you could scale the snow cliff. You have incredible energy.'

These were cliffs with fifty-degree slopes of soft snow. At such a steep angle you couldn't just use a kick step or try ploughing through. First, you had to pierce deep into the snow with an ice axe to support your weight, then find a footing for one step, then another, as you slowly made your way forward. The best place to stick the axe in was at eye level, then, as you lifted a leg, you pushed it in deeper, lightly kicking out to get a foothold and slowly standing up. Things didn't always go smoothly. When the foothold wasn't secure or wouldn't support your weight, you had to gather the snow around you with your feet, tamp it down and then, distributing your weight, step gingerly on to the soft snow, hoping it would support you. It was like risking your life on thin ice. Once both feet had advanced a step you stuck the axe into the snow so that your weight was supported by three points. Then you placed your foot into the hole made by the axe. Distributing your weight as you went, you stepped up trying to keep the foothold from collapsing. You learned that you should never put all your weight suddenly on to the foothold, the trick being to press down quietly, ever so quietly. It was Aizu's first time climbing a steep snow slope like this, yet he had a wonderful, innate sense of balance.

'He reminded me of a snow monkey. He was so nimble,' Doi said.

By now the vegetables were half-cooked, and Noboru tossed in the three kilos of beef.

'Not all at one time,' Yanagisawa intervened. 'It won't cook that way. You've got to put in one slice at a time.'

Noboru removed the pile of beef with his chopsticks and put the slices in one by one.

'I'd rather you said I was an antelope,' Aizu said as he poured sake from the bottle into each person's cup.

'If people were birds they never would think about climbing mountains,' Yuko said this as she came in from the kitchen to sit near the pot on the table. The men bunched together to make room for her.

'Poor birds. They don't know how much fun it is to climb mountains.'

This was Noboru, who was feeling a pleasant buzz from the sake. This couldn't be expensive sake, but it tasted absolutely delicious.

'This guy's fearless,' Ariga said, looking at Aizu.

'No, skiing put the fear in me.'

'Even with a knife-edge you kept on going, so there was no way you could take the lead.'

On the mountains Ariga had cautioned Aizu a number of times to get more serious. By 'knife-edge' he meant when the ridge of a slope is as thin and sharp as a knife. Since both sides were cut away you couldn't use an ice axe. The snow was unstable – hard in some spots, soft in others – and in places there were rocks mixed in as well. Sometimes on a gentle slope you went down a step so you could stick the axe into the slope and hold on to the knife-edge as you went. But if the snow was fresh, it was hard to get a foothold and you had to be extra careful. Packed snow is easy to walk on with crampons, but with soft snow it's hard to keep your balance; if the wind is blowing hard, it can be dangerous. If you happen to fall, the climbers in front and behind need to leap as quickly as they can to the other side. They are roped together to prevent a fall. Fortunately, on their climb, conditions hadn't got that bad.

'Don't stop eating. The meat will get tough if it's overcooked,' Yuko said to the younger members of the group, as she handed each person a bowl with an egg. In the sukiyaki pot the beef cooking in the vegetable broth was quickly losing its redness. Noboru broke the egg into his bowl. The yolk had a line of blood in it, which he ignored as he beat the egg with his chopsticks.

'This is great! Imagine having all this beef!' Aizu beamed as he leaned over to help himself before anyone else.

'Wait for your elders,' Yuko cautioned him.

'It's OK. Those on active duty get priority,' Noboru intervened, transferring some of the beef into Aizu's and Doi's bowls. He sensed how he was growing apart from them. Once he left this party, he would have to construct a new life for himself.

'Remember how beautiful the weather was that day we reached the summit of Kamuiekuuchikaushi? There was no wind at all. The kind of clear day that only comes once or twice each winter,' Doi said, his cheeks stuffed with beef.

'Well, Doi, why do you think we were making those weather maps every day?' Yanagisawa said. 'We listened to the radio report and wrote down the weather systems, adjusting them, reworking the weather map. We adjusted it little by little until we were completely enveloped by a high pressure system.'

'Amazing,' Aizu said, totally absorbed in eating.

'It really was beautiful,' Yuko said. 'I felt so moved when I stood on the summit, so happy I could make it despite all the difficulties.'

Hearing Yuko say this made all of them happy. As they made their way over the ledges with overhanging snow, the sky had grown visibly clearer. They had had to make a big detour to get around the overhangs and were quite worn out. Some areas were danger zones where avalanches were possible, and they had to remain focused. But after passing over several of those, they finally stood on the summit, gazing out over the mountains around them. The mountains were completely white, although each had its own distinctive, subtle shadow. And above them lay a void that could only be called azure. The pure blue sky, full of a limitless energy, flooded the earth below with light. Standing beneath such a sky made them feel like small creatures troubled by gravity, needing to find a way to free themselves from their confines. On the narrow summit patches of snow on the rocks had been carved out by the so-called 'shrimp-tail wind'. The hardened snow, almost ice, had traces carved into it by the wind. Noboru hacked into a patch with his ice axe and gazed up at the sky. He felt he was closer to the sky than ever before. Feeling himself dyed by the limpid blue he felt distilled and purified. This was the most beautiful place he had ever been.

The thunderous sound that had rumbled through his belly still remained, down inside and didn't seem like it was going to disappear. Noboru lay in the depths of the darkness, crushed by unbearable weight. He felt exhausted, without the strength to push back. He scrunched down in hopes of escaping it even a little, but still it pushed down on him. Even as it was hard to breathe, Noboru decided to try to sleep. He could barely move, so sleep was the only option.

Almost without thinking, he began to dig at the snow around his mouth to open up a larger space. There was more air now, and he felt better. Now he could stop and consider the situation. Where was he? The weight crushing down on him not only constricted his breathing but made it impossible to open his eyelids. He couldn't move an inch.

He tried to force his eyes open, but it was so dark he wasn't sure whether his eyes were open or not. Something hard touched his eyes. He had no idea what it was, what was going on. This kind of agony could only come in a dream. The power outside him, crushing him, outweighed the power within him. It weighed on him, and he grew exhausted and sleepy. The road led towards sleep.

He was walking through a green forest that few had entered before. He had to pay close attention or else he would lose sight of the path. In some spots the trail petered out altogether – and, guessing where to go, he forged on, ploughing through the bushes that towered above him. Up ahead, nearly knocked around by the branches bouncing back after they had been pulled aside, continuing unperturbed, was Yuko. She was taking the lead, and since there wasn't a real trail here how she chose to proceed would reveal something about her personality. Yuko tended to forge ahead through the thickest of bushes, even if the footholds were tenuous, always taking the shortest route.

Everywhere there were beautiful, moss-covered cliffs with water gushing out, but when the walkers went on a little way they came to a bleak stream with scattered boulders left by an avalanche or a flash flood. The boulders seemed unstable, so the walkers had to step lightly on them. And, of course, walking up stream beds one had always to check the weather.

Noboru looked at his map to make sure they were at the confluence of the No. 8 stream. Earth and sand had piled up, forming a low but flat shoal. As long as they picked a slightly elevated spot, and it didn't rain, they could pitch a tent there. Where spring avalanches would occur was anyone's guess, but apart from when water spilled over in a waterfall, there was always some flowing at ground level. They took a break under a bakko willow tree and then set off again up the No. 8 stream. It was slightly uphill, the banks sloping away precipitously, and sometimes the current ran strong. Boulders had been washed down from deep in the mountain's recesses, rounded and smoothed the further they tumbled, a process that became more evident as the walkers climbed up from the opposite direction.

They entered a deep ravine hemmed in by cliffs on both sides and could no longer hike on the stream bed, so they went into the forest, trampling down the butterbur along the banks. They couldn't see the ground through the vegetation, which made them hesitate as they chose their steps. It was a clean forest of mostly ezo matsu and todomatsu pines.

Noboru could tell they were at a higher elevation, because the angle of the sun had changed. Taking the lead, he thought about how Yuko might now discern something about his personality by seeing which direction he took them in, but there was nothing to hide any more, no reason to show off. He lost sight of the pink ribbons but forged ahead where he could, always keeping track of the location of the stream. He headed towards the lightest part of the forest, where the trees thinned out only to be replaced by a thicket of bamboo grass as tall as he was. With each step he rotated his knee outwards, parting the grass to create space for his body. He was soon bathed in sweat. There was no wind, which made conditions even more oppressive.

'We should get out of here,' Yuko said, unable to stand it any longer. Her voice melded with the swish of the grass.

'Yeah, I know.' Peeved, Noboru had been thinking the same thing. His backpack got caught in the grass, and it felt to him like being pulled backwards. The grass was thicker than he had realized, and he wanted to get out of the thicket, come out into the stream again and soak in the water. The sound of the rushing water was enticing. He leaped from rock to rock, over the water, the path ahead growing steeper.

As they drew nearer to the waterfall, they could feel the vibration of the plunging water through the soles of their shoes. They were ready to call it a day. Before the waterfall was a snowy gorge. Below the gorge was snow-melt water, flowing fast like an underground stream, and they had to walk extra carefully. The earth seemed swollen, perhaps pushed up by the snow, and they pitched their tent on a small rise.

It would still be light for some time, so as Yuko aired their sleeping-bags out on top of the tent Noboru brought out his fishing gear. He fixed a line to the carbon rod and tied on a hook and a sinker. He went down to a shallow part of the stream. Turning over a stone, he found an insect, which he pinched off and affixed to his hook. He walked upstream, stepping gently, trying to prevent his shadow falling over the water, and dropped his line into a standing pool formed by boulders. He got a bite straight away; the line pulled taut. Noboru hadn't experienced such delight in a long time, and as he held the pole firmly in his hands he took a moment to look up at the sky, bordered by the looming mountains, growing red with the approach of sunset.

Noboru pulled his fishing pole up, and from the water a rushing crystal of light leaped up on the line. A Dolly Varden.

He grasped the trout, which was larger than his hand, and he could feel the beating heart of the mountains.

'We could live up here, you know.'

It was Yuko, standing smiling, pot in hand. 'You want to give it a try?'

'OK.'

Noboru placed the gleaming fish into the pot. Yuko quickly put the lid on it, and the beautiful living being he had caught was out of sight, its presence indicated only by thuds as it wriggled around in the pot. He placed the pot on the ground, passed Yuko the pole, then found an insect and put it on the hook for her.

Yuko got a bite as soon as her line hit the water. As the Dolly Varden flew through the air on the hook, at a loss as to what was happening, it struggled violently. When Noboru took the lid off the pot to add the catch to it the first fish jumped weakly.

'It seems a shame to trick an innocent fish like this,' Noboru said as he adjusted the bait.

'From now on when we come to the mountains all we need to bring is rice and miso.'

'And don't forget the sake.'

'We could have some mountain vegetables, too.'

Yuko kept on catching fish, one after the other. She got her own bait and put it on the hook herself. Eventually Noboru had to stop her, telling her they had caught enough.

Noboru cut open the fish with his knife and gutted them. He squeezed some butter from a tube into the pot and sautéed the fish. He then poured in rice from a retort pouch, added butter and salt and made a pilaff. The fragrance of the

Dolly Varden permeated the dish. Both fish and rice were delicious.

He skewered a Dolly Varden on a branch and grilled it over a fire until it was charred on the outside. To sake he was warming in the pot Noboru added the grilled Dolly Varden. This concoction was an old favourite known as 'mountain trout bone sake'. Noboru took a sip of it, let out sigh of pleasure and gave Yuko a sip.

'Oh, that's so good!' she exclaimed. Like Noboru she loved the mellow taste of the drink imbued with the fatty flesh of the fish.

As he watched Yuko sip the sake by the light of the fire, Noboru felt content. Except for the light from the fire, it was now dark, the edges of the surrounding mountains like faint shadow pictures rising up in the gloom. Tomorrow they would attack the summit of Kamuiekuuchikaushi, although he couldn't be sure which shadow it was.

They were utterly alone. They grew cold and went into their tent, where they undressed. Yuko's skin seemed so smooth, her body fragrance fresh as the mountains. Noboru might very well have been the same. He loved every part of her body. He touched her cheeks, her breasts, her stomach and between her legs. Kissing her passionately, he fingered her vagina, and then he entered her, both from the front and the back. He had the presence of mind to come in her hand. As if imbued with the strength of the mountains, he immediately grew hard again when Yuko sucked him. As long as he was with Yuko, anything they did made him happy. It was too bad that they couldn't fit into one sleeping-bag. Snuggling each into their own bag, they fell asleep holding hands. Noboru woke up several times during the night but never let go of her hand.

They arose with the dawn. After breakfast they carefully sealed away all their remaining food, putting trail mix and raingear into a pocket that was easy to access. They sprayed their bodies with bear repellant, although if they did run across a bear Noboru wasn't sure it would be enough to drive it away. They pulled on their climbing boots, then picked up the bones from their dinner of Dolly Vardens and threw them into the river.

Noboru had climbed this mountain before and knew how difficult a trek it was to the summit. There were three routes to the top. The route to the left of the waterfall was steep, but the path was stable and could be taken safely with a climbing rope. The route to the right of the waterfall didn't require a rope, but there were stones that could fall and injure the second person, if loosened. It was also possible to climb the cliff up through the bamboo grass thicket further to the right, but that would be hard going. None of the routes had what could be called a real path. Noboru and Yuko talked it over and decided to try the middle route.

Yuko took the lead. As she chose her footholds, a faint path took shape. There were no tall trees, just a scattering of birches. Because of the strong winds even the birches didn't grow tall, seeming to hug the ground instead. Using the birch roots as a ladder and the bamboo grass as a rope, Noboru pulled himself up the slope. It was hard to breathe, as if someone were squeezing his lungs from the inside. Every hundred metres they sat down and rested. There was nothing to block the wind, which struck them full in the face. Beyond the green mountains, one range after another stretched off into the distance.

'No such thing as an easy climb, is there?' Yuko said as she sat on the jutting cliffs and gazed up at the blue sky. He couldn't tell if she was addressing him or herself. Noboru passed her the plastic bottle filled with water from the mountain stream. As Yuko drank, the blue of the sky showed through the clear plastic. The water still retained the freshness of the stream. As she passed the bottle back to Noboru, the water sloshed around in it. The further up the mountain they went, they could expect the water to get colder.

'Still can't see the summit.'

'We won't be able to until we get to the valley.'

A U-shaped valley carved out by a glacier with steep rock faces on both sides, there would be plenty of alpine plants in flower there. And Yuko and Noboru would have the magnificent view all to themselves. Just like the *kamui*, long before humans set foot here . . .

They set off again before their sweat had dried. On the shelves along the cliffs were rocks, seemingly set down at random, balanced precariously. If Noboru, who was taking the lead now, slipped he could dislodge a rock that would head straight for Yuko behind him. Other rocks, the size of a human head, looked ready to fall apart if touched. It was like the game *shogi no yamakuzushi*, where you stuck your fingers into a stack of *shogi* pieces and pulled them out one by one without making a sound. If you did make a sound, then it was the next player's turn. This was no game, however. Dislodging this mountain of rocks might prove fatal.

The waterfall off to one side had worn away the rocks and become a stream racing down the slope. In places it clung to solitary rocks and seemed to come to a halt. Noboru, standing still, could make out the dips and projections in the rocks where it would be safe to set their feet and hands. He felt apprehension, but he also felt resolve. One false step and he would plunge to the valley floor below, slamming into the rocks along the way, and die. Death would come quickly, but Noboru wouldn't give in to that temptation. Without thinking he began to move.

No matter how slow your progress might be, conditions would eventually change. Their experience in the mountaineering club had taught Noboru and Yuko this lesson. Yuko, who had taken the lead again, dislodged two stones one right after the other, but both slid down the slope at an angle and missed Noboru. The slope gradually became less steep, and they were able to ascend without using their hands. The water in the stream flowed at a more leisurely pace now, and they no longer had to follow its channel – under their feet lay solid, grassy soil.

The valley suddenly opened up. The first thing Noboru saw was the noble, light pink of the mountain heath flowers. There were clumps of yellow globe-flowers as well. The small, pure white petals of the Aleutian avens were in full blossom. And then there were all the flowers whose names he didn't know. The path wasn't steep at all, now; it was like walking on a plateau. Bright sunlight flooded down from the clear sky, and every single flower shone. This was the hidden heavenly paradise that Noboru and Yuko loved;

where all your struggles and pain would be rewarded. Being here made them happy.

They put their backpacks down next to the stream, where the water gently slapped against the rocks. They crossed it in a single step. Noboru found a boulder he remembered from before and they took a rest there. Back then they must have done the same thing, sitting on the boulder, stretching and gazing up around them. The huge rock ridge, carved out by glaciers long, long ago, before the reach of human memory, stood there – a massive screen. This was Mount Kamuiekuuchikaushi.

Noboru and Yuko looked up at the snowy gorge on the slopes of the ridge and, at the same moment, spotted a brown bear. The same colour and shape as a boulder, the huge animal was far enough away that they weren't frightened. Noboru felt a closeness to it, as a fellow creature sharing the valley with them. About a hundred metres away, the bear looked in their direction. Noboru toyed with the thought that maybe the bear shared his feeling. In this space bound by rock cliffs, there were only three of them through whose body hot blood was pulsing – the bear, Yuko and himself. Even if there were other small creatures about he couldn't see them. In a place like this, even without exchanging a word, he knew that he and Yuko shared the same emotions. A watery, colourless white moon hung in the centre of the azure sky.

Wordlessly they stood up and began the assault on the summit. The climbing trail headed towards the snowy glacier where the brown bear was, but Noboru knew it would get out of their way, and he wasn't afraid. But to play safe Noboru took the lead. At the gorge, just below where they had seen the bear, Noboru looked for a way around the spot. The slope was so steep his nose nearly touched it, and he took each step forwards with great care. There were no flowers here, just dark-green dwarf Siberian pines. The sticky smell of sap filled his nostrils, like the concentrated smell of life.

The snowy gorge where the bear had been was blanker than he had expected, but the animal had left tracks. The slope was incredibly steep. Before he knew it they were almost at the wall of the ridge. Along with pride at having made the summit, Noboru felt an excited rush of blood deep within him.

His lungs contracted and quickly expanded. Breathing hard, he reached the ridge, but the summit was still far off. He crossed over the half-circle of the ridge. Perhaps because of the wind, some of the dwarf Siberian pines came up only to his knees, while some were his height. The view on the other side of the mountain opened up for the first time, spread out far and wide. It felt like standing on the blade of an iron axe. He stepped over the twisted roots of the dwarf Siberian pines jutting out of the earth as he went. Each time he and Yuko took a break they switched who was in the lead. The summit should be coming up soon, Noboru remembered. A swathe of pink lingonberry flowers peaked out underneath the dwarf Siberian pines. Up that slope a little way, the slight swell of ground was the summit. Noboru, in the lead now, stopped and turned around to face Yuko.

'You go first.'

'No way,' she replied, smiling wryly.

'You sure?'

Noboru resumed the same rhythm as he set off again. It was a little harder at the end, but the familiar exhilaration of reaching the peak of a mountain welled up inside. Noboru came to a halt, waiting for Yuko to catch up, standing at a place where he could go no higher. The two stood side by side, silently gazing down at the valley they had just crossed. The bear wasn't there.

As he enjoyed the panoramic view Noboru pulled Yuko close. As if her mind were on one thing only, Yuko closed her eyes, thrust her chin out, her lips slightly parted. Noboru gazed at her lips for a moment, then thrust his tongue deep between them. Anticipating this, Yuko wrapped her tongue around his, put her arms around him, pushing her chest into his. Trying to keep his footing on the narrow peak, Noboru could picture the two of them, clinging together as they slipped down the mountain slope. Even through her clothes he could feel Yuko's frame and flesh – sturdy for a woman. He knew he could always rely on her as the companion he would be with for the rest of his life. Even in the midst of his passion these thoughts ran through his head.

'Nobody else is around. It's just the two of us, as far as the eye can see,' Yuko said calmly. She was right, but Noboru wasn't sure how to proceed standing up like this. It was just the two of them in this world, and no one was there to bother them, but still he didn't know what to do. As Noboru hesitated, Yuko pressed her body against him more tightly.

*

At this moment, as he was unsure what to do next, Noboru came to. He realized he had been sleeping. A terrible weight was pressing down on his entire body. His chest was especially painful. His fingers felt frozen, lacking sensation, but still he tried to dig out space for his mouth. It was pitch black, not a scrap of light. But he could tell that what was pressing down on him was snow. The rumble of the ground came back to Noboru. That rumble, destroying and swallowing up everything in its path, had been an avalanche.

While the six of them were sleeping in their snow hole, they had been struck by an avalanche. He had realized it was an avalanche moments before it struck. Outside was a dark snowy mountain so there probably was nowhere he could have escaped. Noboru lay there, among the debris that had flowed in from the avalanche – tree roots, frozen mud and hard, compacted snow, like ice, very different from fresh powder. Noboru was packed in this, unable to move.

What happened to Yuko? She was alive and well in his dream – but had she escaped the avalanche? And what about Yanagisawa and Ariga? And Aizu and Doi? Noboru was powerless in the debris, but if one of them had escaped there was still hope. If one person could make it down the mountain and contact the climbing club, a rescue party would be on its way. Noboru had no idea if he was face up, face down, or on his side. It was so dark he couldn't tell which way was up.

It didn't seem like he was buried very deep. The lack of light was because it was night. He wasn't optimistic, but neither was he in despair. He was simply there.

'It's an avalanche, so there's not much you can do about it.'

Noboru was about to say this, but he couldn't move his lips because his mouth was obstructed by debris. As he wriggled his hands and feet, shoulders and face muscles he realized he was twisted around at his waist. And he couldn't move to straighten out his body.

'I should have kept on dreaming for a while longer. There was just a little bit more to go.'

Noboru tried mouthing this, but his lips must have been frozen together. If he could have slept a little longer, he and Yuko would have made love at the summit of Kamuie-kuuchikaushi in summer. Why did he have to wake up? He had lost out – and in a big way.

His head ached – to its core. Something must have struck it, but at least he was able to think straight. His next thought was that if his face continued to be crushed against the snow like this he would end up with frostbite. He imagined the blackened faces of the Mount Xuemen victims, the eight friends of Akasaka. If you had frostbite you could cut off fingers, but you couldn't very well do that with a face. Noboru, gritting his teeth and ignoring the pain, forced his fingers into the snow, around his face. They may have been bleeding, but they moved one millimetre, two millimetres, giving him the sensation of blood circulating, even if it was only a little.

He wasn't sure how long it took, but eventually Noboru was able to slip the palm of one hand between one cheek and the snow. His palm was pushing against his cheek, but he could barely feel his cheek or his palm, and they didn't feel like parts of his body. Noboru understood that it was his left hand. Where was his right hand? Did he still have it? He inched his left hand towards his nose – moving it forwards, then back, over and over, until sensation returned to his left cheek. Circulation brought pain, but pain meant he was alive.

His fingers finally touched his nose, where they stopped. His cheek and nose and fingers were wet – with what had to be water. His fingers moved more easily. He was able to feel his right cheek, which tingled. Blood all at once flowed into both cheeks, his nose and his left hand, and at the same time he understood what had happened to his right hand. It was twisted around, behind his back. His shoulder was pinned so he couldn't move his arm. Right hand twisted behind him, his face pushed down – as his position became clear to him, he suddenly felt constrained and cramped.

Steam seemed to be rising from his face. He was losing heat, and as his face got steadily colder he feared it would freeze again. And that would mean frostbite. If the frostbite got really bad, would they have to cut off his head? Noboru smiled faintly at the thought. He became aware of the hood of his parka near his hairline, and after a desperate struggle he was able to get his fingers to lower it to his nose.

He felt pain but couldn't locate it. If it were just bruises that was all right, but a broken bone would be a major problem. Pinned down as he was, he had no feeling in the rest of his body. He was conscious, and he had feeling in his hand and his face. But moving his hand even a little took great effort, and Noboru, completely spent, let gravity pull his head down as if he were apologizing for something. He sensed that he was lying on his stomach. He tried to keep the part of his face not covered by his hood from directly touching the snow. And he began to think about when the avalanche hit. He had known, almost as if he had seen it with his own eyes, that it was approaching. Starting somewhere up on the mountain, mowing down trees that may have been standing for more than a hundred years, ploughing up soil, rolling boulders. An unstoppable force.

Noboru had been frozen with fear, but after a certain point had braced himself for the onslaught that was almost upon him. The entrance to the snow hole easily collapsed, and a burning smell flooded in along with the debris. The smell was from the condensed air, pushed inside the snow hole seconds before impact. The snow hole's ceiling caved in first, and then mud and debris fell in. In other words, Noboru was covered first of all by soft uniform snow. The moment he was buried he felt as if his soul had left his body. But since he was in total darkness, his soul wasn't looking down upon his body.

Noboru pictured his body bruised and torn. Maybe he was under the illusion he was still alive in the debris, but was really dead. His mind was working, but he couldn't hold a thought for long. He was overwhelmed by exhaustion so deep it seemed to hit him everywhere he had feeling: his nose, his fingers, his eyes.

His mental strength depleted, Noboru slowly faded into sleep. For the time being sleep was his only comfort.

*

As they came down from the summit and stood at the ridge, Noboru spotted a dark brown bear at the snowy gorge. He couldn't tell if this was the same bear he had seen before. It might well be a *kamui* who's been in Kamuiekuuchikaushi in the Hidaka for eternity. Occasionally, from afar, the bear would show itself, seemingly indifferent. But it knew everything the two of them were doing. Precisely because it was a *kamui*. They would have to pass near the bear, but Noboru felt no fear. The bear-god had allowed them to reach the peak of Kamuiekkuchikaushi, which meant he had forgiven Noboru and Yuko their presence.

As far as they could see from the ridge, there were no other people in the valley. The grey rocks of the ridge formed two arms that spread wide and supported a verdant terrace which was the garden of the gods. As they came down from the narrow ridge the grey wall rose above them. The slanting rays of the sun formed expressive shadows in the rock face. When they arrived at the snowy gorge, they found their footprints, and those of the bear, but the bear itself was nowhere to be seen, although it had been standing in this spot moments before. They gazed up at the ridge towering above them. Everything was still. The sun was about to disappear behind the rock wall, clouds rushed by and the wall of rock looked like it was about to fall. Noboru glanced around for the bear once more.

They had just set down their backpacks. It didn't seem like it was going to rain, so they decided to pitch tent on a slight rise on the banks of a brook. They threaded the fabric on to the aluminium frame. The malleable aluminium poles allowed them to form a dome. They had to prepare dinner while it was still light. Already the sun was behind the corner of the mountain, and the cliffs looked darkly massive.

'I'll make the *chige nabe*. Spicy soup's the best thing when you're tired,' Noboru said.

'What would you like me to do?' Yuko asked as she pulled the pot and pan out of her backpack with a clatter.

'Not a thing. Why don't you pick some flowers?'

'Sounds good.'

Yuko walked over to the field and disappeared from view as the yellow and white flowers began to sway. Yuko was urinating. Noboru pictured her lowering her trousers and knickers, squatting in the grass with her white rear end exposed, urine flowing, darkening the soil.

Noboru filled the pot with water from the brook. He heated the water, put in some bouillon, then added the finely sliced carrots, daikon and onions they had brought with them in a plastic bag. All he needed to add was the kimchi powder and they would have a fine batch of *chige nabe*. He placed a retort pouch of rice in the hot water to warm.

Yuko had laid out their aluminium tableware on the grass and was waiting for him. 'So, after all that fuss, this is what we end up with?' Yuko said, holding her hot aluminium mug wrapped with a towel. She blew on the *chige nabe* as she sipped.

'Meals in the mountains have to be easy to make.'

'True enough.'

'It's good, isn't it?'

'Yes, surprisingly so,' said Yuko, who proceeded to drink up the soup noisily.

It tasted just the way Noboru had hoped it would. He had done a good job. He ate his rice, sipped the soup and poured some over his rice.

The cliffs, like a huge folding screen, grew blacker by the minute. The top edge of this screen wasn't flat but, rather, a steep, sheer peak. It seemed steeper now than when they had climbed it. The muscular cliffs towering above formed a fortress that, with the coming of night, denied entrance to all human beings. The massive screen-like peak changed even as he watched.

Noboru was hoping that here on this terrace, the playground of the gods, he could take his clothes off and make love to Yuko. But as the darkness came on the wind picked up and the air grew cold. Instead of stripping down he really needed to put on an extra layer.

With the bears nearby they had to make sure their food was secure. He dug a hole in the sandy soil where he poured the dishwater and then covered it with sand. They didn't discard a single grain of rice. All their rubbish was sealed in plastic bags which they then stowed in their backpacks.

They went inside their tent, zipped it shut and lit the gas stove. The tent grew warm, and together with their body heat it was warm enough to be naked. They unzipped their sleeping-bags, laid one on top of the other and snuggled in between them, all warm and toasty. Yuko's skin was warm. As he wrapped his arms around her and pulled her close, her chest and belly tight against him, Noboru felt his strength rising. His penis was hard and swollen. He gently put his fingers between her legs and felt her wetness. He had Yuko lie on her back and spread her legs and slipped his penis inside that wetness. As he lay still, deep inside Yuko, the throbbing spread throughout his body, a pulse inside her that was the only thing moving. Noboru felt like his breathing was in harmony with the imperceptible movements of the massive, dark peak. The peak towered above in the empty sky. Yuko's voice began to rise as she lifted her head upwards. Noboru clung to her neck and began to move ever so slightly, twisting his waist. The image of the rocky peak in the darkness came to him. Then he held still and came for a long, long time. In his mind it felt as if the peak of Kamuiekuuchikaushi trembled slightly, too.

He was having a happy dream. A part of him wanted to stop, but he gave in to the pleasure of the dream. It felt so good to come. Noboru awoke in the midst of this pleasure. He was still half in the dream, the afterglow of his orgasm still with him. He had come in his underpants; he tried to reach out to touch himself and he suddenly remembered where he was. He felt his right arm, twisted behind him, turning even more numb. If he became overly concerned with that he would think of nothing else, so he thought of how he was in a sleeping-bag, actually feeling quite warm and unexpectedly comfortable. The weight still pressed down on him, though. He had no clue how much time had passed, how long he had slept. He was in the same position as before, in the oppressive weight of the darkness. Blood was flowing through him for now, and he could manage, barely, to keep his mind alert; but before too long he might start to freeze.

Noboru might turn into part of the debris. No, he thought, I might already be part of it.

As soon as he came back to reality, the afterglow of the orgasm quickly faded. Yuko is an amazing girl. Thinking this about her gave Noboru strength. What happened to her? His one hope was that she had escaped the avalanche. If she could make her way down the mountain and contact the climbing club, then rescue would be on its way. Would he hear the sound of a helicopter? All he heard now was a buzzing in his ears. What about Yanagisawa? Yanagisawa was such a daring, agile man; Noboru couldn't believe that he, too, was pinned beneath the debris. Then he pictured Yanagisawa and Yuko, both having escaped his fate, spending the night together and Noboru felt a twinge of jealousy. This avalanche might turn everything he had going with Yuko upside down. Ariga, the ever-cautious one, might have escaped as well. Maybe even one of the younger students, Aizu or Doi, had, through some twist of fate, been thrown clear of the avalanche. Noboru couldn't bring himself even to consider that the entire party was gone.

He couldn't move, but he wanted to urinate. He told himself to hold on until he could get out of here. Somehow he had to get his right arm free and turn face up. His body pinned down under the weight of the snow, Noboru tried to focus on something else. To be shut up in a physical body was confining. But as this thought passed through his mind, sadness welled up in him and he burst out crying. His crying echoed back to him right away. This amplified his emotions even more and he cried even louder. Crying didn't help him. I need to be doing something else, Noboru thought, biting his lip.

Using his left arm he dug out the snow around his shoulder. His body heat may have melted the snow for a while, but now it had frozen again as hard ice. Small stones in the debris abraded his fingertips. Every time his fingers came across a rock or twig he carefully dug it out. There was no space to toss what he had dug up, so he carefully laid it beside him. Once he had dug out his shoulder the pressure on it disappeared. He began slowly digging away the snow around his arm. The weight of the debris had compacted the snow, and when he tried to force his way through it hurt his fingers. He thought of himself shut up inside ice.

Noboru pictured a frozen mammoth from the Ice Age. If I end up like that, he thought, maybe it wouldn't be so bad. He took a break as he considered this, then set back to work. He encountered a stone and used it to dig. He dug out his right arm to the elbow, then tried moving his arm. He could feel the circulation returning. The part outside the fleece jacket sleeve, from his wrist to his fingertips, had no feeling, as if it were not there any more. The skin had been directly up against the debris, and he might have got frostbite.

Where exactly was he? He continued painstakingly digging out the debris from around his arm. He shrugged his shoulders, bent his elbow and somehow was able to free his right arm. But he had no feeling at all past his wrist. He grabbed it with his left hand but couldn't feel it being held, and the fingers of his left hand felt like they were touching ice. He dug more debris out of the way so he had room to move his arm and pulled his hand back inside the sleeve of his fleece jacket, hoping that his body warmth would restore feeling to it, if only a little. For a time he lay there without moving, as if frozen solid, and he began to sob quietly. These emotions filled him with a faint yet warm feeling.

He was lying face down, pressed down, but felt he could turn face up if he tried. He was sweating inside the sleeping-bag. There was no doubt they had been hit by an avalanche, but he wanted to know how he stood in relation to the situation. How thick was the layer of debris? If he tried to get free, which direction should he aim for? What frightened him was not knowing exactly where he was. He could no longer hold back the need to urinate. He struggled as much as he could and managed to undo the sleeping-bag zip, the zip of his trousers and pull his penis out of his underpants. He felt beside him to check it was debris, then peed, squeezing out the last drops one by one as he finished. Some of it must have wet his sleeping-bag, but most of it was silently absorbed by the debris. Even the smell of urine struck him as warm and friendly. It must have frozen immediately, for the smell soon vanished. Inside his sleeping-bag Noboru half turned to lie face up and took a deep breath.

Since it wasn't clear for the time being how he could extricate himself, he told himself to calm down. At least he was alive with no apparent major injury. He was lucky. What he needed now was something to dig with – and a light. And gloves. He tried to recall where things were in the snow hole. They had used the gas stove in place of a heater, so the inside of the snow hole had been warm. The ceiling was falling down a little, so they had shut off the stove and climbed into their sleeping-bags. Before that they had used a shovel and saw to cut out a shelf on the wall, where they put their cooking and eating utensils, stove and provisions. He had rolled up his snowsuit to use as a pillow. He had placed his gloves inside his snowsuit so he wouldn't lose them. So what had happened to that snowsuit? He had put the map next to his bed, his climbing boots behind that. But he couldn't recall whether he had put his head-torch in front of his boots or not. He must have put it where he could reach it, so it had to be just above the pillow. Noboru considered all this, although he knew that if the avalanche had swept everything away it was all pointless speculation.

Yuko should be right beside him, to his left. Ariga would be to his right. Yanagisawa would be just past Yuko. Hoping that Yuko and Yanagisawa might hear him he pounded the wall of debris with his fist. It didn't make much of a sound but enough for them to know someone was signalling to them. A low vibration should get through. Noboru stopped pounding and listened. That wind-like sound – could there be a space in the debris? It felt as if all the debris were ringing, but he didn't sense it was a signal from anyone. Noboru turned in the direction where Ariga would be and repeated his pounding, but when he stopped there was just silence.

He shoved at the debris in front of his face, compacting it right and left, and was able to bend his knees, trying to make the space he was in a little more comfortable. But he was merely compacting already compacted debris, forcing himself even deeper into an inescapable place. Finally, somehow, he was able to turn his body, relieving the weight pressing down on him.

As he dug he was slowly able to move his body more.

Still without a single ray of light, he had to feel his way as he went. He began to sweat, the unnatural position quickly straining his muscles. Carving out space at an angle above him was, he figured, the most effective way to free himself. Although if the debris was too heavy this was impossible. There was a hopelessness to his struggle, yet he had to do something.

Lying on his stomach, he rested his arm on his forehead. He may have slept a little. His fingers felt something soft. He was sure it was edge of the sleeping-bag, but it felt different somehow. He dug with his stone towards that softness. He pulled at it, and it stretched, and he realized it was the rubber band that held a head-torch to a person's head. A ray of hope! Tugging at the rubber band, he frantically dug around it with the stone. Before it had been completely extricated he felt around it and found the switch.

Yellow light exploded before him. The snow was radiating light. He had never seen such beautiful snow. The light seemed to shine right through it. The lens of the head-torch formed stripes of light. Careful to preserve the batteries, Noboru switched it off. He was plunged into an even deeper darkness now, yet the shape of the yellow plastic head-torch remained with him. He dug more around it.

He was able to get the head-torch in his hands. He hefted it, checking its shape and weight in the darkness, then turned on the switch again. Light leaped out like fire. There was a name written on the head-torch in familiar handwriting: Yuko Hasegawa. Noboru was struck by a deep sense of dread. The debris was mostly snow, but mud and small rocks and branches had been rolled up in it. Noboru quickly checked exactly where he was situated. He was in a narrow hole with barely enough room for his body. Frozen in the debris beside him was a grey inflatable mattress. The grey looked blurred in the half-translucent debris. That's where Yuko was. Noboru switched off the lamp and turned to the debris, a wall of solid ice. He found a tree root in the debris and used that to dig with.

He attached the head-torch to his head. Once the batteries died he had be plunged back into darkness, so he would have to use it sparingly. With an immediate goal before him, Noboru dug without ceasing, scraping over and over with the root, pounding the wall of debris.

'Yuko! Are you there? Is anybody there? Answer me! Anybody?'

He yelled out loudly at first, his voice reverberating back to him – as if there were an insect inside his head, buzzing. He gradually lowered his voice, called out again, then stayed quiet, but he already knew there would be no reply.

'Yuko! Am I the only one alive?'

The more he cried, the lonelier he became. He was shut up, alone inside the ice. He knew they had travelled up the Satsunai River and were halfway up the slopes towards the ridge along the banks of the Junosawa. Far beyond that towered Kamuiekuuchikaushi. His being able to breathe like this meant there was a dead zone in the debris flow, a gap. Noboru continued to dig, hoping against hope. The mattress slowly revealed more of itself. He pushed it with his fingers, and it softly yielded to the pressure.

He brushed against something cold and frozen, with a shape he couldn't be sure of. He switched on the head-torch, but the light was so glaring he instantly shut his eyes. When he did open them he saw a red hood. The edge of the hood was pulled up to reveal an ear. The frozen, small, delicate ear of a woman.

Filled with inexpressible emotion, Noboru dug frantically. He kept the head-torch on and dug his tree root in above the red hood. A nose became visible. He had no doubt who it was. He dug with all his strength, but he was slowing down. He got up on his hands and knees, sunk in the darkness, and moved his arm mechanically. He tried to clear his mind of all thoughts. Of course he wasn't able to.

Before he realized what he was doing, he was shouting her name. 'Yuko! Yuko!' The voice came out on its own, from the pit of his stomach. A lump of ice, as if leaning in his direction, fell towards him. He tried sticking his fingers into the place where it had been, but the ice was hard. He stayed in this spot for a time, his shoulders heaving. He was in tears.

He had switched off the lamp for a time, but now he steeled himself, closed his eyes and switched it on again. Sensing the orange light through his eyelids, he slowly opened his eyes. Before him, covered in the hood that looked dusted with glass shards, was a face. He lifted the hood, and the glass shards fell away. It was Yuko's sleeping face. Protected by her hood, it did not have a scratch. She looked as if she would wake up if he only shook her. White ice crystals covered her eyebrows and eyelashes. He brushed the ice off her lips. He touched her cheek. Even with the limited sensation in his fingers her skin felt so cold it sent a shiver through him.

He traced her eyebrows with his fingers. White ice crystals flew out, the lustrous black hairs all neatly arranged. Yuko never paid much attention to makeup, but her eyebrows were nicely shaped, the excess hairs plucked. He touched her eyelashes – they were like a line of new grass – and the ice crystals sprang off them. But when he touched her eyelids it was a different feeling entirely; they were hard as stone. Noboru traced the hollows and bumps of her face with his fingers. She showed no signs of pain or suffering. Yuko was finally all his, he thought, and he ran his fingers over and over her face. His mind was lucid, and no tears came.

'Ms Hasegawa – Yuko, I mean – is very tough when she's in the mountains and is a trustworthy leader. She's got an iron will and will take the lead in a snow storm and not hesitate to forge on. And Noboru Odagiri, too, as everyone knows, is a calm and reassuring leader who has overcome any number of hurdles. I've been in climbing parties with him many times, so I know him very well. In the spring climb we made in the Hidaka Range, while we were camped on the ridge at the Junosawa, we were hit a huge avalanche, of unprecedented scope, and the entire party was buried in the snow. With his – I guess you'd say – tenacity, Noboru dug and dug through the rock-hard debris and after three days was able to break free. Then he dug out the rest of us and saved us. Since he saved my life, I'm eternally indebted to him. To tell the truth, I always found Yuko an attractive, even dazzling, person and was secretly attracted to her. But she never knew how I felt . . . Well, um, what I should say is that Noboru and Yuko make a really great couple. They most definitely do. They were before they were rescued from the avalanche, but when they were rescued that really decided it. Noboru beat me. But that's OK. I'm sure we'll be friends for life. Good friends are one of the great blessings in life. To have a great friend like me, to have a gorgeous, amazing partner like Yuko – is Noboru a lucky man or what? Noboru, Yuko – congratulations!'

Ken Yanagisawa then raised his glass of beer in a toast. They all raised their glasses. And almost all of them, following Yanagisawa, drained their glasses. At Yanagisawa and Ariga's suggestion they had chipped in to throw a wedding reception for Yuko and Noboru, inviting only their climbing friends. The couple had simply reported to their parents and relatives that they had got married.

Each of the friends stood up to say a few words when the spirit moved them. Tadao Ariga, wearing the most stylish, up-to-date suit, the picture of an up-and-coming television-company employee – suggesting an entirely different lifestyle from that of Yanagisawa, who was a civil servant – made the following speech:

'I, uh, suppose I'm a little slow on the uptake, because I had no idea that Noboru and Yuko were a couple – even after climbing with the two of them for so long. Yanagisawa was apparently Noboru's rival in love, but I only learned about that later when Yanagisawa talked about it. When I was buried in the avalanche I was unconscious in the snow for three days and three nights and only learned what happened after I was rescued. I never seem to know what's going on and am always surprised when I finally find out. I'm sure you're a little concerned as to whether I can do a good job at the TV station – even when you're a lap behind, there's a point when it feels like you're in the lead as your fellow competitors seem to catch you up from the rear and are just behind you. Noboru and Yuko being together was the biggest surprise in my life. More surprising than finding myself being dug out of the snow. I had just thought of Yuko as a younger member of our mountaineering club, but now here she is married to my friend. Things really change fast in life, don't they? Everything else around me seems to change while I always seem stuck in the same place. Noboru, Yuko, please don't forget me. I'll come over for dinner sometimes, so see you then.'

Noboru wasn't sure if Ariga really was as ignorant as he made himself out to be, but what came through in his speech was what a decent person he was, and when he finished he was given a big round of applause. There are as many possibilities as there are people, Noboru mused. In the cosy bar they had hired out for the occasion Akasaka and his wife and eight men with suntanned faces were also there. The air just around them seemed still.

The next person to speak was Keizo Doi, now in his second year at university. He still didn't own a suit, apparently, and was wearing a nice shirt but no tie. Noboru could tell it was his very best shirt that he had scrimped to buy. Doi stood up straight, and with his voice booming he began: 'I'd, uh, like to take this opportunity to make a confession. I knew everything. I saw Noboru and Yuko in the snow hole exchange a look, and then one went outside and then a few minutes later the other. Yanagisawa saw this happen, too. After they'd gone outside I saw how Yanagisawa was left behind. It pained me to see the mental struggle he was going through, and I felt uncomfortable staying there.

'When the avalanche hit us, I knew what was happening. Not that I saw it coming or anything, just that I knew something was happening and I couldn't do anything about it, and immediately I knew what it was. The avalanche occurred because an unusual amount of cornices had built up at the Junosawa stream and they fell, causing a chain reaction, the wind produced by the avalanche leading to a bigger and bigger avalanche. Mountain birches were uprooted by it, soil rolled up as it cascaded down and the avalanche gained strength. The avalanche started on the main crest near the fork at Mount Satsunai, about seven hundred metres southeast of Mount Esaomantottabetsu, and quickly moved south-southeast towards the fork at the stream. It reached the main part of the Satsunai River, ran south along the river and came to a halt two hundred metres downstream of the Junosawa confluence. This was a major avalanche, with a path two and a half kilometres long.

'The bottom of the Junosawa is quite broad, so normally choosing to bivouac there is an acceptable choice. The problem was the changing weather as spring came on and whether we considered carefully enough the amount of snow that had fallen for several days. It was actually an enormous amount of snow, and we had to stay put. Traditionally our mountaineering club prefers to advance up the streams, since it's less tiring than climbing along ridges. And with all that snow it actually would have been extremely hard to go along the ridge. All the logs left by the climbing club indicate that the Junosawa is safe, so staying there made perfect sense. The route that Noboru decided to take and the spot he selected to bivouac in were absolutely correct. A large-scale avalanche like that, which climbed up all the way to the ridge, was totally unforeseen.

'When I was buried and waiting for someone to rescue me, I thought about all kinds of things. That's all you can do then, after all – think. And the conclusion I reached was that no one had made a mistake. As long as we followed our climbing plan, that was the only route we could take, and bivouacking at that site was the only choice we had. I was only a first year and not in a position to judge. The only thing I could do was observe. If everybody gives their opinion then you'll never form a climbing party. The avalanche was an unforeseen accident, and no one was at fault. I thought all about this when I was shut inside the snow – and after I was rescued as well. There's nothing that could have been done. I apologize for saying these kinds of things at a happy occasion like this wedding. I just wanted to say something while we were all gathered together. Noboru, congratulations on your wedding. You've reached your goal, and I wish you all the best.'

Doi bowed, his expression sunny, as if he had got everything off his chest. Noboru could agree with almost all Doi had said. Noboru himself had replayed the whole incident in his mind any number of times. The biggest issue had been whether he had fully taken into account the connection between the newly fallen snow and the possibility of an avalanche. One could also question whether it made sense to form a climbing party with a female student and two beginners. And why stay at the most dangerous stream in the mountains in spring? People always said, 'In the Hidaka Range in spring never take one step away from the ridgeline.' That's how common avalanches are. The weather had shifted so dramatically, and in addition there had been an unusual amount of snow over the previous few days. As leader, shouldn't he have checked beforehand which places had the highest risk of an avalanche? Climbing up a stream in the Hidaka in spring was far too dangerous and bivouacking there foolhardy. The Junosawa in particular had a history of avalanches, and with all the snowfall on top of that you had to be cautious. If you traverse it you should avoid the stream and go along the ridge. A voice inside Noboru had been telling him this, but Doi's speech had dispersed it. He felt hot tears welling up. But what point would there be to a climb without risk? Even if you don't seek out danger, trying to avoid it entirely would make climbing impossible. The more he pursued these thoughts, the more he arrived at one question: Why did one climb mountains? It was a question nobody could answer.

Ichiro Aizu then rose to speak. He bobbed his head in a quick bow and looked around at everyone with his cheerful face. He took a deep breath, blinked nervously, then began: 'Um, well, I'd like to start by giving you all the snapshots taken inside the snow hole before the avalanche.'

Aizu handed out photos to each of the guests. Noboru and Yuko shared one set. They were the photos Aizu took as a memento that night before they went to sleep. They were all huddled together, looking happy. In one photo Noboru was smiling, but in the other he looked overly serious. Yuko looked the same in both, showing a satisfied smile. Aizu waited for the clamour to die down after everyone had flipped through the photos, then resumed speaking.

'Uh, this was the first time I'd ever skied, and I apologize for all the trouble I caused you. Our leader Noboru must have been irritated, but he never showed it and always waited for me to catch up. If only I had been quicker we might have bivouacked in some other spot, and maybe we could have avoided the avalanche. Maybe something else would have happened to us. I don't know. But no matter what happened, I know the two of you would have got married. Doi mentioned this a moment ago, but I sensed your relationship, too. Falling in love in the mountains is a wonderful thing, because you can know everything about your partner. When you're in a climbing party, any little change in how people act is obvious. I learned a lot from this experience. I may fall in love in the mountains myself – who knows? – and if that happens, I'll follow your lead and try to keep it under wraps. I'll never forget the feeling when I stood at the peak of Mount Kamuiekuuchikaushi. The mountains were pure white with the snow and ice, the sky so blue, with nothing else mixed in. I've never seen such a beautiful blue. It felt wonderful, as if that pure blue had seeped into my heart. I was able to appreciate fully everything that comes with climbing – the pain as well as the joy. And I want to thank you for that. I'm really grateful that you included me in the climbing party. And whenever you want to know more about skiing I'm your man.'

Everyone knew the climb had been the first time Aizu

had used mountain skis, and his comment caused a great deal of playful kidding. The fact was, his skiing had improved. After Doi sat down everyone poured beers for each other, for Noboru especially, who was given quite a lot to drink. They kept Yuko's cup full as well, urging her to drink up, and she grew flushed.

Mr Akasaka was next. He lived a rustic life raising dairy cows, and a suit and tie didn't really suit him. He nodded to the eight suntanned men and quietly, forcefully began to speak.

'Whenever you climb a mountain, you have to come back safe and sound. Otherwise it's too sad for those you leave behind. If you do have to stay for ever in the mountains, other people will miss you for the rest of their lives. But the stronger that feeling is, the more the spirit of the person who was left in the mountains will live on in our hearts. Believe me, you miss them so much. And the more you do, the longer that person's spirit will live. It's because I missed my eight companions so much that they come to visit me like this. I'm sure there are people who love you. I want you to consider their feelings.'

He and Yuko slept a little, side by side. When he switched off the head-torch and they were lying there in utter darkness, Yuko's face was all the clearer within him. He was sure he slept, but he didn't feel refreshed, as if his head were stuffed full of sand. He didn't know exactly where he was, yet he knew he had returned there. He was afraid to turn on the head-torch in his hand.

But with his eyes closed he did switch it on. He could feel the light through his eyelids. He lay there for a time just as he was, but, not wanting to waste the batteries, he opened his eyes to look. As if resisting a powerful force he turned to his side where Yuko lay. Nothing had changed. The more you feel for somebody, the more their spirit stays with you. Akasaka had said this. Akasaka's strong affection for his eight companions had been what called them forth. Yuko slept there peacefully, eyes closed.

'My goodness, why are we in a place like this?'

This was Noboru imitating Yuko's voice. His voice quavered, and it really did seem like she was speaking. Then he spoke in his own voice:

'We're just dreaming. We'll wake up soon and be out of here.'

'I wonder how we can get out of here. I've been thinking hard about it.'

'The key to that might be very simple. I'll find the answer pretty soon, I promise you.'

'Why don't you ask Ariga? He's sleeping right over there.'

Noboru knew he was leading himself on, but turned in the opposite direction from Yuko and switched off the head-torch. He began digging with the tree root. As time had passed, the debris seemed to have hardened, but it might have been because Noboru had grown weaker. His mind a blank, he kept on digging. He had nowhere to dump the debris, so it was like burying himself as he went. The blood was circulating in his hands, causing some numbness, and he would dig a short time, then warm them up in his sleeping-bag. He dug and dug, and he felt a mind-boggling amount of time had passed.

He turned on the head-torch. A small amount of light went into the debris, which had a slight translucence, but most of it bounced back off the surface. He could faintly see Ariga sleeping in the ice, as if he'd been there for hundreds, thousands of years. As if he had no idea that he was asleep like this. The debris here was muddy and hard to see through, but he knew this was Tadao Ariga.

'Just take it easy. Coming over here isn't going to help you any.' Noboru said this calmly, a faint smile on his lips. He wanted to smile more, but something hot began to fall from his eyes and did not stop. He touched it with his palm. It was so hot, he thought he would get burned.

'It doesn't matter if it's cold or hot any more. There's nothing to be afraid of. It's when you're still alive that you get afraid. Just stay like that, sleeping. I won't wake you.'

As Noboru said this, he filled back the debris he had dug up, his tears freezing before they hit his cheeks. Head-torch off, he lay in the pit of darkness. His chest rose and fell as he breathed, and he felt the weight descending on him with it an unbearable sadness. He couldn't contain his despair any longer. He took a deep breath and wailed: '*Uwaaaaaaaaa . . .*'

With nowhere to escape to, he was bound tight by despair. If only he could cut off his hands and legs and throw them away. Being torn limb from limb and dying would be better than this.

He was alive. But he felt a despair he had never known.

*

He scraped away at the debris to make more space around him. The debris hardened further. Most of the time he worked in the dark. He felt hungry and needed to urinate. Being alive is so painful, he thought. He didn't want to use up all his energy, and when his body started to heat up and sweat he stopped working.

I'm definitely going to get out of here, he told himself.

Whenever he turned on the head-torch Yuko was there beside him. When there was silvery frost on the tip of her nose and on her cheeks, Noboru carefully brushed it off with his fingertips. Frost stuck to her eyebrows and eyelashes as well. It all felt metallic, cold and hard. He put his face against hers, pressing his lips to hers. Could the warm pliancy of his lips be transmitted to Yuko's? He stuck his tongue to her lips, but there was no taste or smell. In the fable of the Snow Woman, breathing on someone took away their life. Noboru hoped he could do the opposite – breathe on her and restore her to life.

'Go ahead and sleep. If you sleep, you won't grow older.'

He had seen a movie about a voyage through outer space. The heroine, a young woman, slept more than fifty years in the spaceship, and when she awoke, although she should be the grandmother of the old woman next to her she was still a vibrant young woman. Perhaps where we are, Noboru thought, is a cryostasis chamber in a spaceship. Yuko is asleep as planned, unaware of the passage of time. He was in the same cryostasis chamber, but he couldn't sleep, and would struggle until he eventually froze to death. He turned off the head-torch, and when he kissed Yuko again it felt to him like they truly were on a spaceship voyaging through the darkness.

The instruments are broken, and he no longer has any idea where they're travelling. They're simply travelling further away from Mother Earth, and there is no way they can ever return. Since that is the case, it matters little whether one is sleeping in the cryostasis chamber or awake, although sleep offers a higher chance of survival. The one who was suffering wasn't Yuko but Noboru. And with each passing moment the suffering weighed down more on him.

Noboru came back to where he was. In the depths of darkness. Encased in ice. Lying in his sleeping-bag, his eyes shut, reduced to mere breathing. His body was weightless and he was just here, encased in ice. Even if his breathing were to stop this was the only place he could be. Right here, beside Yuko.

'Today's payday, so why don't we eat out for a change?'

It was the frantic time of morning, and as he buttered the toast that had popped up Noboru looked at Yuko. Her back was to him as she stood in front of the stove, frying eggs in a pan.

'There's no need to waste money,' she said as she transferred the eggs on to a plate. She had fried two, sunny side up, and they truly did look sunny.

'It's not a waste. I think eating out once a month is fine.'

This was the day Noboru's salary was paid by direct bank transfer into his account. All he had to do was go to the bank during his lunch-hour and get some money from the cashpoint machine. His one goal was to see Yuko's happy face.

'I'll make something for dinner. My classes end early today, so I'll pick up something nice on the way home.'

'Buy some red wine, too. No, on second thoughts, I'll pick the wine up.'

'I'll buy it. You always think wine has to be expensive to be good.'

'Maybe you're right.'

'I'll take care of it.'

All he wanted was to make Yuko happy, so naturally he wasn't about to argue over something like the price of wine. Yuko was always quite careful with money, frugal in everything. Both their parents felt they should wait until Yuko finished college before marrying, but they had insisted they wanted to live together straight away, and finally their parents consented.

Noboru was a brand-new company employee, while Yuko was a junior in college. They registered their marriage, but somehow Yuko managed to hold on to her scholarship. They had Noboru's salary, of course, and were doing quite well. But they tried to economize and save. Yuko's idea was that they maintain the same lifestyle whether they had money or not. They wanted to save their money and someday do some climbing abroad. The mountains didn't have to be especially high ones – they just wanted to experience the joys of climbing. Delaying those joys only made them the more precious.

For Noboru, too, if he were given a choice between splurging now by going to a restaurant, where he frankly didn't really enjoy the food, and going climbing abroad in a few years he would definitely choose the latter. Basically, anything was fine for Noboru as long as Yuko was happy. One could say that his putting on a suit and going to work at a company every day was also for her.

Noboru finished breakfast and waited as Yuko got ready, then they left home together. Home for them was the tenth floor of a ten-storey public housing apartment building, one they had won a lottery to move into. In addition to a dining-room/kitchen, their apartment had three rooms, all quite spacious, and the rent was within their budget. They weren't merely paying rent, for this apartment was set up so it would be theirs in twenty years as long as they continued to pay. The apartment was new – not just their apartment, but the hallways, the elevator, the building. Noboru had a good, steady job, and except for Yuko's still being a college student their life as newlyweds was quite ordinary.

The elevator was in use, and they had to wait a while. From the window of the hallway they could see the glitter of a row of identical new ten-storey buildings. The sky was, as usual, clear, without a cloud. They exchanged their usual morning greetings with the slightly older couple that lived on the same floor. Once inside the elevator the high-speed motor overhead whirred. The door opened at several floors on the way down, and Noboru and Yuko said hello to the people they knew by sight. The two of them always held hands, unconcerned about what others might think. The elevator reached its capacity, and some people had to wait for the next one.

In the middle of the well-maintained lawn was a walkway

with colourful concrete tiles. Walking with the crowds down this path, they reached a children's playground, with a fountain shooting water in an arc towards the azure sky. Noboru and Yuko often talked about how lucky they had been to win the lottery. Their married life had got off to a good start.

The colour-tiled path led to a shopping centre, still closed at this hour, and then to the train station. The shopping centre had everything they needed – supermarket, family restaurant, clinic, post office, bank, travel agency . . . The town had so much greenery all around. And the apartment buildings, the shopping centre, the station, the train were all sparkling as if they had just left the factory. As they made their way through the shopping centre this new newly built town started to come alive.

At the train station they slipped their commuter passes into the automatic barrier and went up the stairs to the platform. The train was filled with the soft morning light. Noboru and Yuko sat down next to each other. There were a few unoccupied seats, although not enough to say the train was empty. Noboru and Yuko were able to sit for their commute to work and school.

'This book was really interesting,' Yuko said, in apparent satisfaction, closing a well-reviewed new novel she had just finished.

'Do you think I should read it?' he asked.

'I'd say – yes.'

'OK.'

Noboru took the book, with its brown-paper slip-cover, and put it into his briefcase. He was still in the middle of another book recommended by Yuko. Most of the books he read were ones Yuko had read first. Yuko had already bought her next book to read and took it out of her bag.

'What's that you're reading?'

Noboru was interested since it would come to him next. Yuko showed him the cover and opened the book to the title page. It was only after they married that he found out Yuko was such an avid reader. Newly published books she would buy, while older books she would borrow from the library. She would almost always finish them within the week they were allowed to keep them out, and sometimes Noboru finished them as well. When he didn't he would ask Yuko to check them out again. Yuko read anything she could lay her hands on, and thanks to this she and Noboru had plenty of things to talk about.

As the train began to move, Noboru looked out of the window. The huge, complex stack of concrete boxes was drifting out of view. They passed by large barley fields on a series of gentle hills. Before they arrived at the next station an announcement from the conductor rang out of the speakers, but otherwise the train car was quiet. Noboru didn't have to look out of the window to know what kind of scenery they were passing. It was like a painting.

Finally there were houses on both sides, and the train went underground. The train got more packed with each stop. Yuko kept her eyes down, reading her book, oblivious to her surroundings. Once Yuko began something she remained totally engrossed. Noboru lacked that kind of concentration, although he did tend to block out his surroundings. And Yuko was in that state right now. You might suspect she wasn't hearing a thing, but as soon as their station was announced, she shut her book and looked up.

'I hope you have a nice day. I'll be waiting for you when you come home,' she said with a smile. A faint dimple was visible in her left cheek. Usually it wasn't evident, and Noboru himself hadn't noticed it until they began living together. It appeared when she said something heartfelt, something she truly meant. The discovery pleased him. Happiness meant monotony. The same days one after another, time peacefully passing by, disappearing as soon as it passed. Noboru knew he was living an ordinary life now and was happy.

The university was in the suburbs, and as Yuko got off the train she had to wend her way through people. She wasn't a slender woman, but still she was soon engulfed by the crowds and he couldn't see her any more. The silly thought crossed his mind that Yuko might get lost in the crowd and not know how to get back home. Noboru turned his eyes back to the words in his book. In every word he could feel Yuko's gaze, and it made him happy. Someone else was already sitting in Yuko's seat.

The train stopped in the centre of town. More than half the passengers got off there, and the stifling pressure inside the train was suddenly gone. The company where Noboru worked, not a upper-tier employer like a prefectural government or television station, was a short distance from the centre of town. It was the Hoppo Agriculture Products Company, a small, independent firm with a solid reputation, and Noboru had wanted to work there. Mainly it manufactured livestock feed, but it also had a research facility that was developing dent corn as well as seeds and seedlings for pasture. Good dent corn for cattle required proper soil conditions – calcium, phosphorous and minerals – so the company also did research on fertilizers.

So that Noboru understood the workings of the entire company he was first assigned to sales and marketing. He made the rounds of co-ops and cattle ranches near the city, selling mixed feed and other products. Part of his job entailed working closely with a project team that aimed to mechanize entire farms in order to improve the efficiency. What Noboru really hoped to be involved in was a project in which daily component analysis of individual cows' milk was conducted and the formula of their feed adjusted accordingly. He had in mind a computerized system by which formulae could be calculated and managed.

At any rate, Noboru was happy he could work for such a good company. He got along well with his colleagues, too. He was concerned how he and Yuko would adapt if he was transferred to another region, but so far life was proceeding smoothly.

Noboru didn't know where he was. He was happy to be able to move freely, but he was worried about the weather. He had made all the preparations for mountain climbing in winter, done everything by the book, but now it was raining. And not just raining but pouring. What would normally be a trickle as it ran down the several hundred metres of the rock face was now a huge thunderous waterfall. The traverse route was carved through this wall and thus was impassable now.

Even if it meant a major detour he chose the less steep slopes where the flow of the water wasn't as strong. So he would be climbing up a stream. Along the way was the occasional butterbur. He had never experienced this kind of weather before. Noboru was getting drenched, but he couldn't turn back. The reason wasn't clear, but he needed to meet Yuko up ahead. He had made this climb three times already, transporting food and supplies, so Yuko wouldn't have to carry a thing on her climb. Once he arrived there they would have plenty of food and could pitch a tent and stay for days. As he climbed through the shallow flow, Noboru tried to recall their plan. They would set up base camp in a col safe from avalanches, then climb several of the nearby peaks with a minimum of equipment.

The higher he was climbing now, the muddier and more stone-ridden the water became. He had on raingear, but still the rain seeped in, and he was soaked to his underwear.

The slope grew less steep, the water stopped flowing and suddenly the sky cleared. And before he knew it, it was night. Countless stars glittered in the clear night sky. Yuko, near by, must have smiled, Noboru thought. Hard, packed snow lay beneath his feet. The temperature had steadily dropped, and his clothes were frozen. The moment he asked himself why he had to come here, the wind began to blow, with snow mixed in. No matter what, he had to continue. His limbs were stiff. He needed to draw on more strength than he had ever had, just to go on. He legs seemed to freeze, and he couldn't walk further. He would crawl if he had to, but he couldn't move.

*

He woke up and was happy to find it was a dream. And then slept for a while again.

He slept and woke, slept and woke. His watch told him it was 16 March, which meant that he had been in the snow hole for three days. Right now it was the middle of the night. Not that it made any difference since light didn't reach him. Noboru thought about how people have internal clocks and focused on the area around his chest. It was like wind blowing in a hollow, but he couldn't feel a thing. He moved his focal point to his stomach, his fingertips, his brain, but still couldn't feel anything. As Noboru struggled to keep lucid he realized that his sleeping-bag had frozen. When he had moved his body heat had melted the surrounding debris, but it had frozen again. As he moved his inner focal point through parts of his body, he must have stimulated his organs, for now he had to defecate. He tried to tighten his sphincter muscles, but the internal pressure was gradually building up. What else could he do? Lie on his back, perhaps, to take the weight off his rump, but the moment he relaxed his sphincter what was inside his abdomen emerged. He felt a warmth spread to his bottom and was relieved at first but felt like crying. The foul smell hit him straight away. But when he considered how it came from his own body it wasn't bad. He moved to lie face up and felt something soft around his butt. Facing upwards Noboru urinated.

'I'm sorry. Being alive is so painful.' Noboru faced where Yuko should be beside him and said this aloud. He opened his eyes, but there was just darkness. Everyone in the world must have forgotten about him, he thought. Noboru pictured his mother and father. His father had been working for a company in Tokyo for thirty years. When he had been promoted to general manager, which was when Noboru had been studying for his college entrance examination, they had a small celebration at home. They opened a bottle of champagne and had a special Japanese-style stew, but that was all. His father, his mother, his younger sister and Noboru, all four of them beamed at each other. What had Dad said? 'I made manager, so now it's Noboru's turn to get into college.' It was coming back to him, bit by bit. Noboru got into his first choice of college on his first attempt. And when that happened the four family members again gathered around the table, cracked open a bottle of champagne and had the same special stew. His father must have been following the same routines as his own parents when they celebrated his accomplishments.

On the way home from work his father had bought some frozen headless prawns at the supermarket and tossed a few of them into the stew. He recalled his father saying they were pulling out the stops today. Noboru felt uneasy, knowing that for his father they remained a luxury item. In the bubbling stew the blackish half-translucent prawns immediately turned a milky white with streaks of pink. Noboru, at his father's insistence, began eating them, although he felt like he was staring at a massacre. Prawns aren't that tasty anyway. His father kept tossing more of them into the pot, mixing them in with the already-cooked ones. The three of them told him to wait. Noboru's got into the university of his choice, so next it's Miho turn, his father said happily. Miho would be taking the entrance exam this year. Right about now is when she would be learning the results.

Noboru and Miho were four years apart. His father and mother had planned it that way. So that they wouldn't have two children in college at the same time they had been telling Noboru since he was in junior high that he had to pass the entrance exams on the first try. Noboru's mother was an even-tempered person, always with a smile on her face. Until Noboru was in his second year of high school she had worked part time as a cashier in the local supermarket. When Noboru knew she was working he would avoid walking past the store. When he began preparations for the entrance exam his mother left her part-time job. She didn't say anything in particular about this. It was more like an unspoken agreement within the family. If Miho's entrance exam went well he figured it would be another celebratory stew with his family. His father would probably buy even more prawns than when they celebrated his passing the exam.

His father and mother had a 25-year mortgage on a house in a humble little town along a private commuter line. On the outside there were slight differences among the houses in the area, but basically they were all identical. His parents had bought the house a little later than other couples their age, so they had to choose one far from the city centre – a forty-minute ride on the express train and then the third stop on the local. Noboru always felt that this distance from the city gave the town an abstract feel. This new town had everything, yet had nothing. People lived there, but there was nothing there. And even now his father, mother and sister were living in this nondescript place.

'After I get back from the mountains, I'm going to go

home first of all. Got to try on the new suit Mum bought for me.'

Saying this aloud made Noboru feel like he really would be going home. Anyway I've got to get out of here and walk on my own two legs again, he thought. Being so sleepy like this means my body's getting weak. He checked his watch again. It was more than three days ago that he had eaten the curry rice that Yuko had made. He hadn't eaten a thing since then. He remembered how good it tasted – the potatoes, carrots and onions and the small hamburger steaks tossed in at the end. At this rate, he would only grow weaker and not have the strength to dig himself out. He would die of frostbite. The thought made him panic. The head-torch was attached to his head, but he didn't turn it on; instead he grabbed hold of the forlorn little root and began desperately digging into the debris. Perhaps compacted more now, three days after the avalanche, it was as hard as ice. He felt like a bug living in a hole. He faced upwards and dug, hitting something hard. He dug with his hands for a time, then switched on the lamp. It was an ice axe. He slumped back into the debris. Why am I so tired? He had almost no feeling at all below the waist. His faeces and urine were frozen solid. I might be frostbitten down there, Noboru thought, hastily turning off the head-torch. He was wasting the batteries.

Digging and resting, digging and resting, he finally unearthed the duraluminium-and-wood ice axe and hugged it. It was too long for the space he was in. Since Yuko and Ariga were near by that meant there should be plenty of equipment around. He tried to remember where they had placed their equipment and utensils. In the confined space he started digging with the pointed end of the axe. He could use only his upper body, but it was a far easier to dig through the debris with an axe than with a tree root. Noboru recalled definitely having set the axe outside the snow hole with the skis. The avalanche must have crushed the snow hole and rolled it all up. Noboru was alive not through his own efforts but through chance. As he dug around the head of his sleeping-bag he grabbed something hard yet soft, something he couldn't identify by touch. He shined the head-torch on it and saw it was his map in the plastic case. Just what I need. He wanted to laugh. He did laugh aloud, and then sobbed.

When he listened carefully, he felt he could hear the wind. And the sound of some people walking around. He counted the scattered footfalls and came up with eight people. Eight people – the eight people with darkened faces who often gathered at Akasaka's. The dead have more inspiration than the living, and they must have known that he was buried here and come to rescue him. What he thought was the wind was the sound of shovels digging away the debris, and the sound of feet. Eight people working as hard as they could. These older members of the climbing club were, indeed, people you could count on. If you go climbing, make sure you come back. That was Akasaka who said this, but where was that? If you don't, it's too sad for the people left behind. He had said this in the wedding party Noboru had dreamed about, and now was here to rescue him. People who die in the mountains never really intend to, so it's just too sad. It was Akasaka's words, Akasaka's voice.

'Seven people, all roped together, fell to their death right before my eyes, and I was the only one left behind. We were on a forty-degree snow face at the time. I had no idea what to do, and all I could do was descend. Two hundred metres below, there should be two climbers who were suffering from altitude sickness and one medic. I had screamed to them that the others had fallen. It was snowing, so all traces of our path up were gone. I turned around, grabbed the ice axe in both hands, stuck it into the snow, lifted one leg, stamped down with my climbing boot to make a foothold. I followed the cast-iron climbing rule always to keep your hands and feet in contact with the snow at three points. When the foothold was hard enough I took one step down, but the snow under my feet collapsed, and I held on to the axe for dear life. If I were to slip I'd fall, and then I'd never get back. I thought I didn't mind dying, but still I was scared. Being so scared I had no strength in my legs, which gave me a taller profile and less stability.

'On the way down the snow wall I had to traverse crevasses covered over with fresh powder. I stabbed my axe into the snow, searching for safe spots. No matter where I stabbed, the axe slipped deep into the snow without resistance. It was really dangerous because the fresh snow hid the crevasse. Keeping my weight on my back leg, I inched the other leg forwards. Right then I was sucked down into a crevasse. I fell up to my waist but was able to keep from falling further. I kept stabbing my axe into the snow, finally locating a spot that could hold my weight, and I lifted myself up. I had no idea where I would cross the crevasse. I could finally make out the other members of the party waiting below. I stabbed my axe into the snow yet again, and right then I slipped and fell into something like a basin. My backpack got caught on the edge of some ice and somehow I came to a halt. I could see the bottom of the crevasse, perhaps ten metres below. Fall there and I'd never get out. If I continued to slide I wouldn't stop until I reached the glacier way down below. The layer of snow beneath was mushy, and if I stepped on it I'd fall, but the layer on top was nearly ice and I could get a purchase on it with my axe. I tried to get a foothold on the crevasse ice but kept slipping. My weight made me slip forwards little by little. The more I struggled, the more I fell. I was frightened out of my wits. This is how people die. When I was enjoying the mountains I thought I wanted to die here some day, but when you're face to face with death it's terrifying. Just then a clump of snow slid down right near me. Barely keeping my balance I shouted for help. It was all I could do. Before long a man from the team below approached, step by step. I could see the basin-shaped crevasse from where I was, but because a metre of fresh powder lay on top of it the man couldn't see it from where he was. If he stepped on it he'd fall, just like me, into the crevasse. There was only one choice left to me. Death.

'As soon as I accepted this choice, a feeling of calm came over me. Since nothing but death lay ahead of me, struggling wouldn't help. Twenty-eight years of life have brought me to this, I thought. This is the last stop for me on earth. I could see the path in life I'd taken to get here. I couldn't make out the sky because of the falling snow, but I felt calm, as if softly embraced by a clear blue sky. I found it strange that I'd feel like this. And I also felt relieved that I could accept this. At peace, I now heard a roar like thunder. I saw a flash of lightning. This was the apocalyptic end of the world, but it didn't look that way to me. I was at peace, and I felt blessed.

'The man inched forwards. Don't come. If you step on the snow you'll fall. Don't worry about me. I said this desperately, but he held out his ice axe for me. In a daze I reached out and grabbed it with both hands. With all his strength he pulled, but he couldn't get a secure foothold. The more I pulled, the further I slipped into the crevasse. He came closer, as close as he dared, and reached out a hand. I clasped it, and he yanked, but still I couldn't get out. Finally he held out both hands. My foothold was in soft snow and couldn't support us any more. We would either fall together or be saved together. I wanted to live, so much I felt like crying. I struggled to find another foothold, finally got a purchase on something and was able to drag myself half out of the crevasse and, with two hands, grab his wrist. I struggled to get the rest of me out. This was my last chance to live. He leaned back and my whole body was lifted out. He kept pulling. I was out. And the two of us collapsed on to the snow.

'We couldn't catch our breath for a long time. The falling snow flashed silver in the lightning. The pounding of my heart was louder than the thunder. The man hadn't witnessed the any of the climbers falling, but he was aware they had died. I'm sure he felt he couldn't just leave me in the lurch when he saw me slipping away, but I believe what was at work in him even more was the sense that he didn't care if *he* died. I had felt the same way. When I returned to the everyday world, how was I going to explain what happened to people, let alone to the families of the dead? I'd escaped death, but maybe it would have been better if I'd remained for ever in the mountains with my companions. These thoughts raced through my mind. The two of us eventually struggled to our feet. There was no thunder, no lightning. The sky was full of the gathering dusk. I have no idea, even now, if there really had been any thunder. I stood up, and decided to live. But we still had to descend to our Camp 5 at 6,900 metres. Later on I learned that things were pretty bad at the camp, snow swirling with nearly zero visibility, and lightning flashing horizontally across the sky. That alone created a dangerous situation. The axes buzzed with an electric charge, sending blue-white sparks out of the blades, and anything metal – the crampons, the metal fittings on the tents, even the frames of goggles – could not be touched. They sat huddled in the middle of the tents, horrified at the reports coming over the radio. This is what it felt like to know everything that was going on yet be helpless to do anything to put it right.

'The mountain was quiet now, and the two of us began our descent. Finally we got to the camp where the other two members of our party were. They'd dug a hole to get out of the wind and looked in good shape. The four of us began climbing down, almost unable to see our own feet in the increasing darkness. Our route up the mountain had vanished, and we had to carve out a new route. On one side were crevasses on the other snow overhangs we might easily collapse. Climbing backwards now we barely cleared the overhangs. Often the snow at our feet gave way, making us more afraid. When you have the will to survive you're exposed to all the dangers of life. I wanted desperately to live. I couldn't see where I was stepping any more and switched on my head-torch. The camp shouldn't be so far from here, and I called them on the radio to give us the location. For a while, in the midst of the ever-falling snow, you could see torches glimmering. I was surprised how close they were, but they were below us by quite a distance. There were ropes we'd fixed in place on our climb up that we should have been able to follow going down, but we searched and we couldn't find them. Without ropes we had little chance of making it down such a steep slope. The camp could see our head-torches, but it was so dark around us they couldn't give us instructions. Just being out in the snow in darkness like this was a huge risk. I remembered the steep slope on the climb up, but there were similar slopes all around, and I couldn't determine which was the one we'd come up. If we took the wrong route we'd never get back. I stabbed the axe into the ground before me and then shone my lamp around us. I caught a glimpse of red. It was the climbing rope! I had this feeling that something was leading me in the direction of living. We followed the rope down the steep slope. I wanted to recover the rope to use later, but it was too dark, and besides I was running out of energy.

'When we reached the gentler slope, I looked up and saw, through the falling snow, several climbers making their way down the mountain, their shapes vague. The other three people with me saw them, too. The thought occurred to me: These are the climbers who slid off the mountain. Somehow they managed to stop their fall and were coming back to us now. It made me so happy to see them, and I felt a surge of energy. But then they vanished from sight. The snow started coming down harder, and it was a total white-out. When I shone my light, it just bounced back at me from a pure white wall. It was too dangerous to move from this spot. We were able to make contact with the camp by radio, but they were beset by the same conditions as we were. Still, a rescue squad set off to find us. The temperature had dropped so quickly that the ice wall where we'd set the rope on the way up had frozen solid, with twenty centimetres of fresh powder on top of it. It was useless, and we didn't have another one, the rope lost with the climbers who fell. All the rescue squad could do was to wait at the foot of the ice wall.

'We were cornered. We didn't know our position, and trying to get down in the dark was extremely hazardous. We'd have to bivouac, but the weather was turning worse, with a snowstorm and the temperatures dropping to minus 30 degrees Celsius. We were above 7,200 metres, and the air was thin. I learned later on that a large winter cold front was observed at 5,500 metres with a temperature of minus 35 degrees, so at 7,200 metres we might have looking at minus 45 degrees. Each metre-per-second of wind lowered the wind chill by one degree, so with the wind whipping us the way it was we would have been at minus 60. We'd reached the limits of what a person could survive. And you have to remember how high up we were. Altitude sickness, when you're physically exhausted, can disorient you, making you liable to do anything. If the risk had been slight I would have tried to make it back to camp, but this was no slight risk. We really couldn't move from where we were. We dug at the snow with our ice axes to carve out a hole to bivouac in.

‘Fortunately we found a crack in a crevasse. The four of us crouched down, huddled together and shut our eyes. The snow did not let up. At this rate we might be buried in snow and disappear from the face of the earth. I kept my head bowed, as if I were apologizing, and tried to tough it out mentally. My body was being battered by snow and wind. I had to shake myself constantly. The other three kept their eyes shut and didn’t move. They might have been asleep. A little sleep could restore you and was a good thing. I tried to doze off myself. In the morning we’d know which direction to go in. And then we could start moving.

‘It became lighter out, all around a glittering white. The snowstorm seemed finally to be reaching its peak, and the weather looked like it was going to get even worse. I realized I had some rations with me that I’d forgotten about. But I didn’t feel hungry. I knew we couldn’t hold out much longer. My body started to tremble. The other three were shaking, too – the kind of trembling you can’t control. My teeth were chattering. We’re going to die like this, I thought. Before much longer, though, the clouds parted, and we could see the shadow of the mountain in the white-out. This was our final, final chance to make it out alive. Encouraging each other, we staggered to our feet. We were contacted by radio from camp: the rescue squad had recovered some of the climbing ropes we’d set and they were climbing up to us. I couldn’t keep standing; my legs buckled and I slumped to the ground. I couldn’t stop shaking. My body didn’t feel like my own any more. The dark outline of a person appeared out of the snow and got steadily clearer, and I remember somebody putting his arms around my shoulders. My memories are disjointed.

At that altitude my brain was barely functioning. I had to take one thought at a time, like moving one foot forwards, then the other. It felt like somebody else was telling me to move my arms and legs. I did finally make it to the camp and collapsed inside a tent. Somebody gave me a cup of hot milk tea. It had lots of sugar and tasted fantastic. They took off my climbing boots and socks. I was amazed, since my feet were frozen white, a little translucent, like ice. My toes were like mineral crystals. They heated water in a pot, and I stuck my feet in it. I couldn't feel a thing. I have no idea how hot the water was. After a while I could feel, faintly, blood starting to circulate in my feet. It hurt like hell.'

Thus ended the long tale Akasaka had whispered to Noboru. Now, all Noboru could hear was his own breathing. The sound of the men's feet and shovels, the rescue squad, had vanished. He couldn't even hear the wind.

'Akasaka had been at death's door more than once, so that's why he always senses the presence of the dead.'

Noboru spoke this aloud. His voice echoed in his skull, but after the reverberations stopped there was only silence. Noboru felt like he had died once, too, because of the avalanche. He had come back to life, but he was little different from a corpse now. At the very least, everything below his knees was white, like wax. He had no feeling, so everything below his waist might be like wax. If he didn't soak in hot water soon the cells would start dying.

But these thoughts didn't make him feel agitated. Sleep was winning out over thought. He took a couple of deep breaths and fell asleep.

*

The sky was so blue he felt sucked in by it. There was no wind, perhaps because the low-pressure system was gone, and it was the kind of day you had maybe once or twice each winter if you were lucky. Noboru was skiing smoothly along a gentle slope. As soon as he passed the leafless trees they vanished completely, as if they had fallen over. The slope went up now, and Noboru took one firm step after another with his skis. He came out on a sunny plateau, like a terrace. There were several snowy mounds there. It was such an unsettling sight that Noboru came to a halt.

And that's when it happened: One of the swollen snowy mounds began to shake, cracking open, and a person stood up from it. It was Ken Yanagisawa, in full winter climbing gear.

'What's wrong?' Yanagisawa asked, a worried look on his face.

'Well, what's wrong with *you*?' Noboru asked, equally concerned.

'Don't you know the cast-iron rule of winter climbing? If you run into a snowstorm you climb into a survival tent and go to sleep. You'll keep warm that way, and while you're asleep the storm will pass.'

Yanagisawa was grinning as he spoke, and Noboru was relieved.

'Hey, everybody get up. The lost Noboru is found.'

The mounds began to move, and one by one, as if they were hatching from eggs, Tadao Ariga and Keizo Doi and Ichiro Aizu appeared.

'So you're all OK,' Noboru said, smiling.

'Nothing to worry about,' Ariga said, smiling as well. 'Everything's right on schedule.'

But one person was missing. Noboru looked from one face to the next. 'Where is Yuko?'

'Wasn't she with you?' Ariga replied, still smiling.

'What happened to her?' Noboru asked loudly.

'Didn't you take her somewhere?' Yanagisawa said calmly.

Doi and Aizu, beaming, looked on.

It wasn't such an arduous climb. Noboru and Yuko had picked Mount Rakko because it combined both the challenge and the pleasure of winter climbing. It wasn't that high, only 1,472 metres, but still this was the Hidaka in February. Noboru had climbed it as practice when he was in college. There was a risk of avalanches, so they didn't follow the Menashunbetsu River, the normal path for summer climbing, and instead followed the ridgeline. The problem was the accumulation of snow. Since Noboru could take only five days off, including Saturday and Sunday, they couldn't very well wait for the weather, so, checking the forecast on the radio and keeping a weather map, they had to go for broke. If the weather cooperated they should be back after one night and two days. They would use up their supplies as they went along, so their load would get lighter each day. They had brought along five days' worth of prepackaged food. Noboru would carry anything especially heavy.

They had taken the night train from Sapporo to Obihiro and then a taxi as far as they could go. The snow-removal zone ended six kilometres before the Mount Rakko trailhead, so that's where the climb began. They were equipped with brand-new plastic climbing boots that Noboru had bought with his winter bonus, as well as new custom-made skis. The skis took getting used to. And because the skis were touching snow for the first time snow sometimes stuck, perhaps because of the way they had been waxed.

The path to the mountain was a gentle slope, nearly flat. On one side was a pasture, on the other a ranch. There were ruts in the gravel road from four-wheel-drive vehicles and only a narrow area to ski on. Noboru took the lead. It was slow going at first, but soon he got into a rhythm.

Noboru could tell from Yuko's breathing that she was maintaining the right pace, not overexerting herself. They continued up from a dark stream of water that split the snow. He could feel on his cheeks how the temperature had fallen, even though the stream hadn't frozen, which he found odd. When they took a breather they were enveloped in the sound of the rushing stream. Snow came sheeting down from the grey sky. Today should be the last day of bad weather. The weather forecast said a high-pressure system would be moving in tomorrow. They started off again before they got too cold. A forest surrounded them now. And the snow got steadily deeper.

They noted the sign for the trailhead, and they got off the logging road. A snow bridge – a natural bridge made of snow – crossed the darkly flowing river. It was clearly strong enough to bear their weight, and they skied across with no problem. When they got to the other side, the wind picked up, the snow striking them from the side. The ridge they would ascend towered above them. Noboru checked their position again on the map. As the fine contour lines indicated, the slope rising abruptly up in front of them was a 45-degree incline that almost deserved the name cliff.

'We're finally able to come here, just the two of us,' Noboru said, removing his skis. 'Before in winter we were always part of a group.'

'Relationships in a climbing party are a tricky thing, aren't they? The junior members have their place, and the leader is always the leader,' Yuko said as she retied the laces of her snowshoes. She seemed relaxed, which set Noboru's mind at ease.

'So let's never argue, OK?' he said.

'Who's the leader now?'

'In the mountain, or at home?'

'This *is* our home.'

'That would make you the leader.'

'OK, then.'

Her smiling face was beautiful to Noboru. Forming a climbing party with strangers was tiring, but with Yuko, his wife now, this was a family outing.

They stuck their skis upright into the snow like grave markers and took the ski poles in their hands. The ridge they were going to climb was wrapped in snow and invisible. There must be a storm on top, for the wind sounded like cloth ripping. This wouldn't have bothered him in the past, but now he was climbing with family fear clutched at him. This was a feeling he had grown to have over the last year.

Naturally Noboru took the lead most of the time as they ploughed their way through the snow. They had always worn Japanese-style wooden snowshoes, but Noboru had decided this time they would try aluminium ones. They didn't have so much equipment as when they had been traversing, so it wasn't such a burden to carry something more bulky. What he wanted were shoes that were good in deep snow. Yuko had never used this type of snowshoe before, but she was surprisingly good with them. You stepped on to the slope with the tips of the snowshoes, making sure of your foothold. On the bottom of the shoes were metal spikes, so if you put your weight down and gripped with your toes there was no danger of slipping. At first it was just a flat, smooth slope, devoid of trees. If you lost your footing you would fall all the way to the bottom. You wouldn't get hurt; you'd just tumble all the way down. Halfway up Noboru halted and breathed deeply, his shoulders heaving, and Yuko took the lead. Now it was much easier going for him. Whenever there was a gust of wind he lowered his head and held his ground. When he stepped forwards he was careful not to be blown over. Yuko halted, her whole back hunched over, and Noboru quickly took the lead again.

The snow on the ridge was deep. The surface was hard, but if you broke through it you would sink up to your waist in it. Their snowshoes had a large surface area, but often, if you leaned to one side, your feet would sink in. If you struggled too much you would get tired out, so if you fell over you just pulled your foot out and tried again. All Noboru needed to do was choose the highest point to walk on. That way they wouldn't get lost.

The forest was a mix of all kinds of trees – katsura, linden, maple, ezo matsu, todomatsu – and arguta vines. There was a huge amazing oak that spread its branches in all directions. The trees were asleep. The silence of the forest was the silence of sleeping trees. The bamboo grass, too, crushed by the snow, was sleeping. Once spring came and the snow melted greenery would burst forth from the branches, and the bamboo grass would shoot forth, forming a thicket too dense to walk through. Walking the ridge was, in fact, possible only in the winter. Wind blew the snow up from below. The direction wasn't steady, and snow swirled from right and left and then blew away.

The long slope ended, and they went downhill for a short time. As they repeated this pattern the elevation increased, while the trees around them became slightly shorter. A gust of snow blew past, and then, like a curtain having parted, blue sky appeared. Beyond the valley they could see the folds of the mountain, dyed in snow. Through the treetops they saw a couple of familiar-looking peaks. Mount Rakko was the one on the left, partly hidden.

Occasionally they couldn't help but sink into the snow, but generally they found walking with the snowshoes through the forest steady going. Noboru felt himself perspire, but his skin didn't feel damp. Around the largest trees the snow had caved in a little, the warmth of the trees perhaps melting the snow and absorbing some of the moisture. If you stepped there, you sank into the soft snow, and could see the green bamboo grass buried beneath.

They arrived at the forest line at the col around three in the afternoon. Noboru had enough energy to want to forge ahead a little, but they were in no rush, so he followed Yuko's suggestion that this hollowed-out spot, shaped like a saddle, would be a good place to pitch their tent. And

Yuko was right. Even if there were a snowstorm, if they were snowed in, this was a safe spot because there would be no avalanches here. Even if there were a three-day storm it was unlikely that it would continue for a fourth day. If they rationed their food they could make it an extra two days.

Yuko was an active member of the college mountaineering club and one of its leaders, so Noboru, who had already graduated, was obliged to follow her instructions. He dug out a hard flat patch of snow for the tent. The snow would melt in the area around of each person's body, but doing a careful job of preparing the floor made the difference between sleeping well and not getting much rest. They tied the ropes around nearby trees to position the tent. They set the pegs deep in the snow and had to pound them down hard. They then inflated a mattress, laid out their sleeping-bags and sleeping-bag covers on top. In less than thirty minutes of silent work Noboru and Yuko were done.

Inside the tent was their own little world. They turned on the gas grill, filled the pot with snow and heated it until the water was boiling. They placed pouches of curry and rice in the hot water. At once the pouches were covered with silver bubbles that looked like so many fish eggs. There was no wind outside, and the bubbling water sounded like a babbling brook.

'Kind of late in the day for me to say this,' Noboru said, 'but I love being in the mountains. Away from the cares of the world.'

Grabbing two stainless-steel mugs Noboru reached

outside to scoop some snow. He poured whisky into the mugs from a plastic bottle. Cheap whisky, but it tasted wonderful.

'The mountains aren't like those temples in the olden times, you know, the ones women used to seek refuge in,' said Yuko, slowly bringing the mug to her lips.

'Yes, but the mountains are what keep us going.'

'You're lucky. You have the mountains, and you have a wife who loves the mountains.'

'You can say that again!'

The mug felt cold against his lips. The whisky was chilled, but it warmed him.

'Let's not talk about school or work. We're above all that here,' Yuko said, not pressing the point. She seemed to be enjoying the whisky, too.

'This is our own heaven,' Noboru said. 'I wonder what they do in an ordinary heaven. Listen to music, drink tea, chat with people, go for walks – awfully boring stuff. That's why Huckleberry Finn said he didn't want to go to heaven. I think I'd be bored out of my mind, too.'

'This is heaven, all right, but if we just sit around we'll die. And then it'll be hell.'

'Tomorrow let's pitch our tent at the furthest edge of the forest. There's no need to rush or hurry back down the mountain, so let's take our time. And then we can attack the summit. Of course, depending on the time, we can switch things around.'

As he spoke Noboru twisted the dial on the radio, and they listened to the weather report. He crouched down and filled in the weather map. Yuko watched him as she sipped her whisky. A high-pressure system was moving in, and tomorrow would be a calm, fine day.

'Let's try for the summit first,' Yuko said. 'I want to stand on the peak when the weather's the best.'

Noboru could sense the passion in her eyes. The cold tonight would be a drawback, but at least they would be alone. There would be *kamui* on the summit of this winter mountain.

'I think we should have kids pretty soon,' Yuko said suddenly.

Her words caught him off guard. 'Kids? Then we wouldn't be able to come to the mountains any more.'

'Not necessarily. When the baby's small we can bring him in a carrier. They start walking before you know it. And when you get old he'll carry you on *his* back. Let's have a baby, OK?' Yuko stared at him with moist eyes.

Noboru was about to look away but forced himself to hold her stare. 'A baby? Well, I guess we're the right age. You really want to?'

'Yes. Right now.'

Unable to hide her happiness Yuko unzipped the sleeping-bags completely, spreading them out like two quilts. They would sleep on one quilt and cover themselves with the other, but it was a bit cold to get completely naked. Real *kamui* wouldn't mind the cold, no doubt. They would go ahead and make a child. They started kissing, and Noboru saw how Yuko was already perspiring. Impatient, Yuko helped Noboru out of his trousers, unfastening his belt. Noboru did the same for her. Fearing that fingers would get lost in the hem of her shirt and the layers of underwear Noboru headed straight for the valley between her legs. It was hot and dripping. Yuko was grasping Noboru's still forlorn penis, pulling back the foreskin and rubbing the hole at the tip. Their tongues entwined.

Noboru turned Yuko to face away from him and peeled off each layer of her clothing – trousers, underlayers and knickers. He touched her valley from the back, from the front and grabbed his now rampant, jutting penis with his left hand. He slid his right forefinger out of the damp ground of the valley, brought his penis to it and thrust forwards. Yuko let out a cry. He reached around and cupped her breasts, fondling them and feeling the tip of his penis touch her womb. After repeated thrusts the entrance to the womb opened and Noboru came with all his might. Even as he was coming, he drew on strength from deep within him, in wave after wave after wave. After spending himself completely, he grew weak and he clung to Yuko. His shrivelled manhood slipped from the muscles of the valley's damp ground and was expelled.

He pulled the covers up and, as if grabbed by sleep, fell into deep slumbers.

Noboru woke in the morning to Yuko's shaking his shoulders. His first words were: 'Did you get pregnant last night?'

'Don't be silly. You can't tell that quickly.'

'You're pregnant. I'm sure of it.'

It had felt so good not using a condom. Until we know she's pregnant I wouldn't mind doing it every day like this, he thought. Making a family feels so good.

For breakfast they had rice and natto beans, accompanied

by miso soup, all prepacked. The more they ate, the lighter their load became, which made him happy. They left the tent as it was and set off with just a daypack. It was the same scenery as the day before, although clear, without a cloud in the sky. Noboru's mood changed. They walked along the ridge, with valleys on either side, with wall after wall of snowy mountains beyond. Visibility was excellent, and they could easily determine their position.

They walked on silently. Yuko might already be pregnant, and he needed to take extra good care of her, so Noboru always took the lead. The snow was as hard as the day before, but if the temperature rose during the day it might get softer. Before that happened he wanted to get out of the forested area where the snow was deep. They were up so high now there were no large trees, mainly just short mountain birches dancing in the wind. There was frost on the bare white branches, and with the azure sky as backdrop it seemed that there were silver flowers proudly blooming, sparkling in the sun. The frost formed a path, leading the wind on, swelling up on the leeward side. Even the thinnest branches were crystallizing.

When they left the birch woods with their frost flowers, they were near the furthest edge of the forest, and all that lay ahead were two flat mountains of ice. They decided to climb the first and head along the ridgeline to the other, which was the summit of Mount Rakko. The daypack held just chocolate, a camera and a vacuum flask, and when they took out the crampons it became so light Noboru barely noticed he was carrying it. They removed their snowshoes, stuck them in the snow and changed into crampons. They laid their ski poles down and switched to ice axes. On the climb ahead there was the danger of falling. If they fell they would need to stop their fall by swiftly stabbing their axes into the snow. Otherwise, depending on the angle, they might fall where there was no forest to stop them and they would end up at the foot of the mountain. By the time they got there the soft, vulnerable lives of their bodies would be over.

From a distance it had looked like a mountain of ice, but what lay at their feet was snow. Noboru's feet sometimes broke through the snow, and he would find himself deep in it. One metre down, beneath the snow, the dwarf Siberian pines were unexpectedly green, with a fresh scent of rising sap. There wasn't a cloud in the sky, but the wind swirled up the snow. As he trudged up the slope, his iron spikes taking one step and then another, the snow below him became more compact. Every three steps he turned around to check on Yuko. And every time he did so, the word 'pregnant' sprang into his mind. When their eyes met Yuko's crinkled in a smile. Noboru turned back and took another step, thrusting his ice axe into the snow. The axe was tied to his waist, so even if he slipped the axe should hold him. He made sure to always have the ice axe and one foot touching the ground.

It had seemed as if there were two peaks, but when they arrived there was just a ridgeline. The wind was blowing. Countless wind-lines ran through the hard snow, as if they had been chiselled. Above the white snow lay one mountain after another, as if continuing for ever. If you looked carefully, beyond them was the blue ocean. Go all the way to the sea, and you would be in a whole different world.

They edged closer to the windward side of the ridge. A treeless flat steep slope fell away to the side. They chose their steps carefully. Noboru tried to control his pounding heart, checking his footing carefully before moving forwards. Now he was turning to check on Yuko after every second step.

The slope became treacherous, the surface snow almost as hard as ice. The crampons held well. In the final analysis you had to depend on your equipment. He dug the ice axe in, testing several spots, and pulled himself forward. He took out the climbing rope and tied himself to Yuko. He didn't expect to fall, but this way he would be with Yuko whether they lived or died. The final slope to the summit was hard going, his breathing came so hard that his lungs felt as if they were going to burst, and he took each step with the utmost care. Yuko looked like she was having a difficult time but managed to smile none the less. The oval summit was drawing nearer.

At the final spot, where the slope ended, Noboru came to a halt. He turned to Yuko and said, 'I'll let you have the honour of reaching the summit first.'

'Let's go together.'

Yuko took three or four steps at a time and now stood beside him. Noboru untied the climbing rope and grabbed her outstretched right hand in his left. Side by side, they reached the peak at the same moment. He let out a shout.

On the summit was a clump of solid ice twisted by the so-called 'shrimp-tail wind'. They used their axes to break it apart, revealing the wooden sign marking the summit of Mount Rakko. They were at the highest point around them. Cape Erimo jutted out to sea, splitting the ocean in two.

They knew it was the Pacific Ocean, but it looked more like a mountaintop lake. The sea near the summit of Mount Poroshiri, the celestial sea where sea lions frolicked and seagulls flew, might be right around here. Kanna Kamui, who wanted to see the water flowing and made his way upstream to the source of the river at Mount Poroshiri, might have been a salmon, Noboru thought for a moment. He glanced over at Yuko and saw her entranced by the majestic view, so he kept quiet. From the clouds that had formed over the sea, light shone through, golden powder pouring down on to the surface of the sea. But where they stood was even higher.

'I really hope you're pregnant,' Noboru said, gazing out at the distant sea.

'I feel like I am.'

Yuko was looking out at the same spot. It felt to him like she had suddenly aged.

He wanted to live. Yuko was waiting for him back home, and he had to make it back. He stabbed away with his ice axe, digging out debris. Rocks and pieces of wood were mixed in with the debris. The axe bounced off the roots of a birch. The debris was as hard as ice, and lying back in this unnatural position he couldn't gather much strength and the digging didn't progress. Besides, the weight of the debris was compacting the mass, hardening it even more. He could use only his arms and upper body, and his muscles were soon exhausted. Lying face down, immobilized, he felt his body quickly grow cold. Even his sweat began to freeze.

When he couldn't stand the cold any longer he grabbed his axe once more. Without gloves his hands were so cold he couldn't feel whether he actually was holding it or not. In the light from his head-torch his hands and fingers were white as ice and there were ice crystals on his fingernails. He stuffed his hand into the fleece pocket but had no sensation beyond his wrist.

The light from his head-torch seemed to be growing weaker. Lying still in the dark, he felt his heart beating. His beating heart was all he could count on. Face down, unmoving, he felt despair, broken by fear. He knew he was going to freeze to death. The spark of life would burn in him just a few days more than in his companions – Yuko, Ariga, Yanagisawa, Doi and Aizu – that was all. Soon it would burn out. Perhaps it was karma – sins from the past – that made him suffer longer than the others. It would be better if the hole he found himself in had collapsed and immediately crushed him to death, but instead the debris had become hard as rock, allowing him to survive. Noboru could picture the contrast between his small, insignificant self buried beneath the avalanche and all that surrounded him – the mountains deep within the Hidaka Range – Poroshiri, Esaomantottabetsu, Kamuiekuuchikaushi. The wall of debris covering him was probably five metres thick, no more than twenty at the most in spots. All he had to do was break free. He looked at his watch and saw that four days had passed since the avalanche had roared down and buried him. Today was 17 March.

'Yuko, you have to survive. You have to get out of here alive. You're going to have our baby.'

He said this aloud, but his own body could barely move. Only his back moved as he breathed. He wanted to see Yuko and edged back in the darkness. He had dug so hard, but had advanced less than one metre from where he started. Feeling his way, he pulled away fragments of the debris. The debris he had broken into pieces was starting to freeze in clumps. Painstakingly, with numb hands, he tried to break them apart again. His hands came upon something with different texture, and he switched on his head-torch. It was Yuko, the same as before. The contours of her face as sharp and clear as porcelain that had been fired in a kiln, Yuko lay there, eyelids closed, lips together, sleeping. Noboru touched her face, her finely formed nose. She looked thinner, even more beautiful. She was such a pure-hearted young woman. Noboru brought his lips close to hers, stopping just before they touched. It felt to Noboru that if he kissed her Yuko would melt into water and vanish from his sight.

'Yuko, you have to come back to life. Because you're having a baby.'

Noboru said this after he had turned off his head-torch. He held her face in his arms. He wanted to hold all of her, but the rest of her body was buried beneath the debris.

'I'm so happy I met you.'

Noboru's voice bounced back off the wall of snow and the mass of debris, coming back at him from all directions. After the echoes, there was only silence.

'You had a cute chubby little baby girl for me, didn't you. You did such a great job.'

Noboru was at her side, in a white room redolent of

disinfectant, as Yuko was giving birth. Yuko's pain was his pain, their joys were shared joys. The labour pains had been going on for ten hours. All that time Noboru had shared in the same pain Yuko felt. He almost felt as if he himself were on the delivery table.

She had no idea how long she had been in labour, although she could clearly understand the passage of time in her internal clock. At least now that the foetus had dropped lower in her womb the weight and pressure were less oppressive. Even with her lying on her side her abdomen jutted up. She had lost a sense of physical balance, and her lower back was stiff. It was as if there were a taut string inside her body, and the base of her groin was being yanked by it. The foetus's movements were getting less noticeable. She had practised the breathing methods over and over at antenatal class and had read many books on the subject. Her doctor and her husband had told her there was nothing to worry about, but she was so worried she couldn't bear it. She was so frightened she didn't know what to do.

Yuko, wearing a short white delivery smock, was lying on the delivery table, legs spread. The doctor peered between her legs any number of times. Noboru stood beside her, holding her hand. Every time Yuko turned her helpless eyes to him he told her, 'Don't worry. I'll always be here to protect you.' Wave after wave of contractions rolled over her. It hurt so much it felt like her back was going to rip apart. As she had been taught, she took short, quick breaths, focussing her attention on her breathing. As soon as the pain receded, her body, tense without her realizing it, relaxed. She had been taught that unless she conserved her stamina she wouldn't have the strength needed at the crucial time and the agony would be prolonged.

In the whole of human history, what number will my baby be? Yuko wondered as she lay on the delivery table, covered in sweat. There was no reason she couldn't do what untold numbers of women had managed to do in the past, but maybe she would be the one exception. The contractions began again, and it took time for each one to subside. She felt as if she were ready, a little bit, for the next surge of pain. When the pain did hit, she took a deep breath, followed by a series of short breaths. There was a clear difference now between the waves coming in and when they receded. When they receded, she took a deep breath and saw them off. These waves came and went endlessly. But these were just the surface waves of pain and didn't indicate that the foetus was moving. When the labour pains came she strained despite herself but kept some strength in reserve for the final push.

She opened her eyes, and Noboru was there beside her, as always. They looked at each other and Noboru smiled. Just as Yuko smiled back a huge wave hit. She took a deep breath, hoping to ride the wave, but it receded, leaving her behind.

She let go of Noboru's hand and grabbed on to the metal crossbar above her. Her hand was sweaty. She was able to brace herself for the next onslaught but wondered if she could endure it. She felt as if she were drifting in a fragile little boat on the vast ocean, but the baby about to be born must feel even more fragile, born into an unknown world. From the immeasurably vast ultramarine ocean, full of immeasurable love, the baby was trying to make its way into this world, passing through the tiny portal of motherhood. Full of hope – or was it desperation?

Yuko, too, had at one time passed over the sea, made it through the mother's portal and been born. In some distant memory, so distant it made her dizzy, Yuko herself had been bobbing, her body limp, in this sea where there was no rain or wind, none of the pain of birth yet upon her, at peace. She had no idea how long she floated there, oblivious of time. Free from worry, only needing to exist.

'All right, take a deep breath now. Inhale. Exhale,' the nurse said, wiping Yuko's forehead with a damp gauze.

Following her instructions, Yuko took a deep breath. Her face, her chest, her back, her waist were all bathed in sweat, and she could feel rivulets of sweat running down her spread thighs. The world was beginning to move. Her womb was contracting, sending the foetus out into the world. The waves of pain became the rhythm of her breathing.

'That's it. You've got it. Don't strain, relax. If it doesn't go well this time, do it again. That's it. Good job. Inhale, exhale.'

The nurse demonstrated the breathing as she spoke. Unless Yuko concentrated really hard, she couldn't see the nurse's face. She felt a dense, thick feeling of water flowing. She heard a sound like something spraying between her legs.

'Good – your waters have broken. Now you don't need to hold back. Now you can push.'

The doctor's strangely cheerful voice came from below. She heard water splashing. She couldn't see the doctor, or even sense him there. She listened carefully to check whether her breathing was regular. In the background she heard the sound of waves. Yuko was floating in the ocean in that little boat. She was rowing with both hands, with the iron bar above her bed. The boat bobbed up and down, and she didn't know where it was headed. Occasionally she felt as if she were about to faint, and she tried to keep going. The boat rolled, rolled again and then rolled way over, almost capsizing. Something was setting out on this little boat. The waves lifted it up, dropped it down, flowing onwards towards this world. Need to ride those waves. A wave came. A huge one.

'You can't go to sleep! Keep your eyes open. Don't close them.'

A shock ran through her cheeks, first the right, then the left. She thought the waves had slapped her, but it was the nurse who had slapped her. Her cheeks didn't hurt, though. Along with a pain in her abdomen, welling up so much it almost made her faint, a raging wave pushed forwards, enough to cover the sky in darkness. And that wave spilled out of Yuko. Her legs fixed apart, she grabbed on to the iron bar above her. She was tossed about by the wild wave, about to lose control, not knowing what she was doing. White bubbles rippled noisily on the surface.

'You're doing fine. Just relax. You can push as much as you want.'

The nurse sounded close, yet far away. Yuko had missed the wave, but another one came. She faced the wave straight on and let it strike her; she inhaled deeply, breathed regularly and held her breath. But she was still under water and she couldn't keep breathing. She wanted to take a breath but couldn't. She struggled to the surface, broke through, gulped air and felt a little better. Then she tensed her lower abdomen.

'That's the way. Good job! Try one more time. OK – *once more*!' the nurse nearly shrieked.

The wave receded, and Yuko was left behind, all the strength drained from her. She felt as if she were about to be sucked in by an overwhelming sleep, and the nurse slapped her again. Her cheeks were on fire. The next wave was about to hit. As the wave roared down and crashed into her, Yuko took a breath and held it in. Consumed by the wave her body spun around – and, sinking, she managed to let out half the air in her lungs and pushed. She was about to pass out.

'You got it. Good job. Look! You can see the head coming out.'

The nurse placed a hand mirror between her legs so Yuko could see. From a round five-centimetre hole deep within her she could see the dark hair of the head emerging. The hair was whorled. The head was struggling to pass through the final gate from that world to the first gate into this one.

'Don't give up on me now. Work with the baby.' The nurse consoled her, admonished her, guided her.

Yuko waited for the next wave, which would be the most powerful of all. A brand-new person was rowing out into this world. The wave swelled up, rising higher and higher.

This time she had to catch that wave. The new person, and Yuko, both rode it.

'Like a dog in summer, a dog in summer. Relax.'

As she had learned in birthing class, as the nurse told her, she breathed lightly, like a dog panting in the summer heat. *Ha, ha,* Yuko breathed out, praying the delivery would be as easy as a dog's. She felt hands busy at work between her knees. Something slippery was coming out from deep within her. Yuko grabbed the crossbar tight with both hands, breathed out in short bursts and glanced over at Noboru. He was like an apparition.

'We're almost there. Just a little more. A dog in summer, a dog in summer.'

Breathing as she had been instructed to, Yuko felt as if she really had become a dog. All the strength drained out of her. And just then another huge wave struck.

She could barely make out a cry, like that of small animal that had been captured. The cry slowly grew louder. She was so exhausted her eyelids felt like they would shut on their own, but joy also coursed through her being. Yuko wanted to sit up and make sure of what had just occurred, but she lacked the strength.

'Congratulations. I'm so happy for you. It was a completely safe delivery. You have a healthy baby girl!'

The nurse held up the baby, newly arrived in the world, to show her. The child, arrived from the far shore of the sea, was wet and wrinkled. For the baby, its eyes still shut, the world had yet to open. The umbilical cord, like a cable through which signals were sent from over there to here, was cut and dangled from the baby. The inside of the baby's bawling mouth was red. Yuko reached out to take her child but pulled back when the nurse told her firmly she couldn't touch her yet.

Yuko slept. She sank down deeply, as if she herself were becoming the sea. Her pain had long since faded, and she slept a contented tranquil sleep. The waves that came and went had quieted. She wondered who could have woken her up. She wanted to stay in this viscous serene sea for ever, but the tide had suddenly begun to move. This slow movement, at first almost imperceptible, gradually sped up. She was still lying down, asleep, but she knew everything. The tide turned into a torrent she couldn't resist. The moment she decided to let it carry her away, the rushing current stopped. Yuko floated there, giving herself up to the water. Head down, rolled up into a ball like a foetus, Yuko was, until not long before, a fish. She had been contentedly breathing in the water. Before she was a fish she had been some other living creature long, long ago, a being whose shape she wasn't sure of. Before that, a single cell. Before that, an unformed element. And even before that she was a formless thing that existed, yet whose existence couldn't be determined, as insubstantial as a shadow. As it had so many times, the tide turned once more. Floating on the water Yuko began her journey to another place.

'Thank you so much. You did a great job,' Noboru said. 'I don't know how to thank you. You did something I could never manage.' He felt as if he had been on a long, long trip and had now arrived. In the pitch-black space the head-torch off,

Noboru smiled. He moved his mouth but his lips and tongue were frozen and numb.

'I was beside you the whole time, and I was so moved by it. We really had a baby, didn't we?'

He could see Yuko in his mind. Like a small creature that had been rescued from danger, she was gently smiling, still haggard from her delivery . . . Noboru kept on talking. The silence that seemed ready to suck him in was too terrifying.

'Everything's fine. No need to worry. It's a baby girl, just like you hoped for. She's a little underweight, so they've put her in an incubator. They control the temperature there. It's bright in the incubator, but it's warm so it's like the baby's still inside you. She's sleeping peacefully. They wrote your name in magic marker on the soles of her feet, and I almost got the feeling it was you back when you were a baby. Everything's fine. She'll be able to leave the hospital when you do. We have to think of a name for her. I've thought of a few already, but we can talk about it later.'

Noboru said all this, but his mind by this time was a blank. His energy was fading fast. His lower half might be frostbitten, for he couldn't feel a thing down there. So frozen he couldn't tell if he was in or out of the sleeping-bag. He wanted to grab the handle of his axe, but his hands wouldn't work.

He was trying to survive, but he couldn't. He would dig out the debris, then sleep, sleep and go back to digging, getting slightly closer to the outside, but it didn't get a bit lighter. At some point, his watch had stopped, and he no longer knew what time it was, what day it was. Thoughts of death grazed his mind, and he thought of his father and mother with whom he had lived all his life. His mother and father had no idea he was about to die here, buried under debris.

He thought he would write a final note to leave behind. If by some chance he were to be rescued, it would be something to read again and laugh over. Even if the others decided that Noboru and his group had run into trouble and sent out a rescue team they wouldn't be in time, and it would be impossible for them to locate this spot. Once it got warmer and the snow melted their six bodies would be discovered. If they found his note, then at least they would know that he had survived for a few days and had tried his hardest to live. This would be Noboru's testimony that he had been alive in this world.

He had thought the map wouldn't be of any help, but the back of it was blank. And a mechanical pencil was sticking out of the fleece pocket of his parka. He took the map out of its plastic folder. At the confluence of the Junosawa, he had written '13 March: Camp'. Four days had passed since then. He wanted to believe he was pleased to have survived these past four days. Noboru turned the map over. His head-torch was only giving out a dim orange light now. Noboru was certain that when the light went out so would his life.

On his stomach, Noboru remembered how he had studied like this when a child, and he took the wrinkled piece of paper and began writing. In the fading light, squeezing out his last ounce of strength, he wrote:

> 14 March (what day of the week was it?): At early dawn we were hit by an avalanche while sleeping in the snow hole. There's debris all over, so it must have come in from the entrance.

I woke up in the midst of debris. There was a space around my mouth so I could breathe. I dug out more space, enough for me to move around a little. Thanks to the head-torch I was able to see my surroundings.

I found Yuko Hasegawa in the debris. Her face was like she was peacefully sleeping, as if she died without knowing what hit her. Next I found Tadao Ariga. He looked peaceful, too. I think the others, too, must have died instantly.

Because I survived I accepted my situation and tried my best to be rescued. I know it's all in vain, but still the time I spent here was very rich for me. I say this because

At this point, Noboru was utterly spent. He barely had the strength to switch off the head-torch, then rested his face on the back of the map and slept. There was so much he wanted to say, but his hands wouldn't move. Noboru felt himself fortunate to have survived, even in a state like this. He was able to live with Yuko, whom he loved. These few days had been like a lifetime. He could marry the woman he loved and do what needed to be done. He had to believe that.

Man's life is like a dream. He was so blessed to have met Yuko. If the two of them knew about their life together, that would be enough. That is what Noboru was thinking when he woke up. He felt stronger, although only a little.

He switched on the head-torch and the filament in the miniature bulb glowed like a weak ember. He brought the light close to his piece of paper and, clutching the mechanical pencil, began to write.

Mother, Father, please forgive me for being a bad son and dying before you.

This struck him as a cliché, but he had no energy to rewrite it. Unable to move the pencil with one hand, he placed his left hand on top of his right to guide it. The pencil point pierced the paper, but he didn't care and kept on moving the pencil.

I don't know how to apologize for having this kind of incident take place just as I was on the point of entering the company and repaying all the kindnesses you've shown me. As I dug away the snow, I came across an ice axe and I was so happy because I thought that I'd be able to get back home to you, Mum and Dad, but I wasn't strong enough. I can only imagine how sad you'll be when you learn the child you've raised so lovingly is dead. Even if I am destroyed, I will always be by your side, watching over you. You'll sense me there sometimes, and at those times I really will be with you, watching over you.

I did a terrible to thing to them all – Ken Yanagisawa, Tadao Ariga, Yuko Hasegawa, Keizo Doi and Ichiro Aizu. I'm sure people will say all kinds of things later on, but all the responsibility lies with me, the leader. The other members are entirely blameless. When I think of the pain the bereaved families will go through, it is hard to bear.

Even if all the members of our party go on to the other world, we will always be together. And that mountain – I can't remember the name – we'll climb it together.

Miho, you'll be taking the college entrance exams this

year. When Mum and Dad hear about this accident they'll be in shock. You're the only one they can count on, so please take good care of them. And please forgive your brother for his irreparable mistake.

Mr Akasaka, thank you. Your words are haunting me now – that we shouldn't die in the mountains. That it's too sad for the people left behind.

Thank you to everyone who's ever helped me.

With these thoughts I end my life in this world.

Noboru had to rest five times while he wrote this, fighting off the desire to sleep. Holding the pencil in both hands, he used every ounce of strength he had left as he wrote the words, one by one. Writing had never been so painful, as if he were carving each word into stone. At the end he wrote the date, March 17. The battery on his head-torch was running out, the light visibly fading. His life was about to vanish, yet Noboru didn't feel driven into a corner. A burning fire is eventually extinguished, so too with the fire of his own life. That's the way things are.

The filament in the miniature bulb was just a dot and then it vanished, as if sucked into the darkness. And even afterwards Noboru continued to write his final message. He had to write it all down while the words were still in his mind.

He couldn't lift his head any more and lay face down on the map. He couldn't feel his lower half, and now he couldn't feel his stomach, back, shoulders and arms. He couldn't feel the fingers of his right hand holding the mechanical pencil.

'Thank you, Yuko. Thanks to you I had a wonderful life.'

His lips were the last thing that moved. A peaceful feeling overtook Noboru, and he sank into sleep.

They were walking on a logging road that ran along the Nukabira River at the upper reaches of the Saru River. They had left their daughter in the care of someone, and it was just the two of them, Noboru and Yuko, in the mountains. This road was under the management of the electric company, and they had had to park their car quite a long way back. This was the trail up to Mount Poroshiri. At 2,052 metres Poroshiri was the highest peak in the Hidaka, and as one of the official hundred famous peaks in Japan it was known for the crowds of climbers in summer; but for some reason it was just the two of them hiking down the trail. What Yuko saw Noboru saw, what he thought she thought, so there was no need for them to exchange words.

They walked silently down the dry white gravel of the logging road, lined on both sides by greenery. There was a slope so they knew they were rising in elevation. A clear stream near by kept up a constant babble. The woods rang with the calls of birds. Their feet made no sound on the gravel. Instead what they heard was the wind blowing from treetop to treetop. Bathed in greenery, they walked along, feeling utterly refreshed.

The logging road petered out at a concrete hut, a water-intake facility owned by the electric company. After that a vague path branched off along the right bank of the Nukabira River, a path beaten down by people walking through the grass. With each step they were getting deeper into the mountains. Soon the valley closed in on them, and they couldn't go along the stream any more, so they walked through the stream itself. On top of a boulder they changed to boots for hiking up streams, ones lined with felt on the soles to keep them from slipping. They stowed their climbing boots in their backpack. The boots for hiking up streams, with their rubber inner booties in place of socks, seemed somehow light and unreliable.

They leaped from boulder to boulder, as cliffs rose up on both sides of the stream. Where the water was shallow they jumped on rocks just below the surface. The felt soles had good traction, even on the wet boulders that were extremely slippery. Cold water soaked their ankles. Where there was space between boulders they splashed through the water. Suddenly they were both wearing shorts. This was cooler, and with their backpacks weighing them down, they found wading through the water easier than leaping from one boulder to the next. The mountain stream twisted, curved, formed eddies, its flow complex. The speed of the current was different on the surface from on the bottom, and they had to brace themselves so as not to be swept off their feet.

The stream angled off and light shining through the branches made the water sparkle. The spray from waterfalls glittered. The stream was ever-moving, constantly transforming. The water dyed the rocks on the riverbed a light green. You could tell it was water because it was flowing, but if it ever stopped you could no longer distinguish between it and the air around it. About to leap to the next boulder, Yuko scooped up a handful of water to drink, and Noboru did the same. The water was cool and refreshing as it ran down his throat. The water had the quintessential smell of the mountains.

They entered wetlands that ascended in steps up a slope, water spilling over them and flowing downwards. Each shelf was a hollow, the water still and clear. As it flowed down from there, the water formed countless silver threads. Yuko and Noboru skirted the edge of the vessel, climbed up a small waterfall and on to the rock shelves.

They were steeped in the smell of water. There was a spot where they had to wade up to their waist, getting their shorts soaked. Holding hands, they crossed the river, supporting each other. The shadow of an occasional fish would flash by. A yamame trout, perhaps, or a Dolly Varden trout.

They scrambled up and down large boulders that had been washed down during a rainstorm when the stream had turned into a rushing torrent. The boulders had raced downstream with a deafening roar, crashing into each other, rebounding, breaking. There were indeed times like that. Once the rain in the mountains stopped, though, the current would settle down again and the boulders would come to rest. The river wasn't a muddy one to begin with, and over time the water would once more run clear.

From the Poroshiri Lodge they ascended the mountain stream, and sitting on a boulder, they changed into climbing boots and trousers. The path ahead was a tough slope up through the forest. The winding dirt path had been trodden by many feet. Other people might well be walking it even now, but they saw no one else. The forest here was completely different from the forest path below, with its broad-leafed trees – Japanese elms, oaks and katsura – for here it was all conifers – ezo matsu and todomatsu. The woods had a dignified fragrance. Noboru and Yuko weren't on a hurried schedule, and they climbed at a leisurely pace, each making sure the other was doing all right.

Finally they emerged on to the ridge. To the left of the steep cliff they could see the north valley that had been carved out by a glacier. Angular boulders cut out by the glacier were scattered about. The triangular peak beyond was Totsutabetsu. The climbing path was a rocky trail curving through the dwarf Siberian pines. On either side were fields of flowers. The pink sack-like flowers were *ezo* cherry, the white ones with a touch of green were blue cherry. There were white flowers – Aleutian avens, chickweed, liliaceas, yellow cruciferae – as well as chishimafuuro and ezohime kuwagata. There were countless flowers in bloom, so many you would need a guidebook to identify them all. But the names that people happened to assign to them didn't mean much. This was a secret field of flowers in full bloom. The field of flowers continued on and on, its beauty helping them forget how hard they had climbed.

Shrill, metallic cries echoed around them. These were tiny rodents – pika. They peeked out from in between rocks, with whiskers and curious expressions, totally unafraid of the two humans in their midst. They stared at Yuko and Noboru, their eyes all dark pupil. Once they determined the humans were safe these light-brown rodents clustered to their right and left, in front and behind them.

There were still several snowy patches. Flowers would

bloom there once the snow melted. Drifting clouds threw the snowy patches into shadow. When the wind picked up, the flowers trembled, showing the path of the wind. Pika boldly scampered around the base of the flowers. Their cry – the distinctive *piki piki* – sounded like singing. These tiny creatures might very well be angels.

The ridge trail wound around the valley. Once the pika were gone, Yuko and Noboru were surrounded by utter silence. The vista was magnificent, and they almost regretted having to go on to the summit. Step by step they climbed and before long reached the gravelly summit of Poroshiri. They weren't breathing hard at all and weren't perspiring.

One mountain after another stretched out before them. They turned to the southeast and saw a magnificent, imposing peak soaring upwards. This was Kamuiekuuchikaushi. Once, during the time of heavy snows, they had had an idea to pass along the peaks of Kamuiekuuchikaushi and Esaomantottabetsu, make a base camp at Mount Kamui and aim for the summit of Poroshiri. Then they had run into an avalanche and couldn't complete their plan, but now at long last they could. They gazed out at the mountains in silence. There was nothing to fear, just beauty all around them.

They could have stayed there for ever, but without a word they turned back from the summit. There was a place they had to get to.

They walked along a ridge of rocks. There were dwarf Siberian pines all around, clusters of tiny red pine cones in the midst of the dark green needles. The trail disappeared, and they continued along through the chest-high pines, the ridgeline their only guide. They couldn't see their feet so they stepped cautiously. They passed another mountain peak as high as Poroshiri, then a number of small peaks like the serrated edge of a saw and clambered down a steep slope. There were no dwarf Siberian pines here. They were on sandy gravel. They turned around, and there was Poroshiri, towering majestically above them. Despite the patches of snow on the slope, it looked like the back of a huge black bear. Water originating here became the Nukabira River, then turned into the Saru River and flowed into the sea.

In front of them rose Mount Totsutabetsu. It was easily recognizable by its clear-cut three-sided pyramid shape. In the valley to the east several swamps glistened like jewels, each one reflecting the sky. This was Seven Swamp Valley. With Noboru in the lead, they slowly descended the precariously piled cliff of rocks. They needed a climbing rope, but Noboru felt strangely light, his body buoyant. The valley grew steadily larger before them. It must be these swamps on Mount Poroshiri that Kanna Kamui arrived at, following the water upstream, climbing the mountain to arrive again at the sea. Here were seagulls and sea lions, the water filled with an abundance of seaweed.

He took his time clambering down the cliff and came to a snowy patch. He used his kick-step technique to make his way through the hardened snow. Silence was everywhere. He couldn't hear the crunch of snow beneath his feet. As they walked along, side by side, their strides were in perfect harmony. They stepped from the ring of snow on to damp earth. They headed towards the water, taking care not to trample the multi-coloured flowers surrounding them. They stood facing the pellucid water. There was a white beach at their feet. It had been winter when they set out from the foot of the mountains in skis, and now the seasons had changed and they had finally arrived. The wind picked up, and they could hear waves lapping at the shore. They gazed around, wondering if a white bear would amble into view.

Also published by Peter Owen

www.peterowen.com

NATSUME SOSEKI (1867–1916) is Japan's most revered writer and one of the great writers of the twentieth century – described by the *Sunday Telegraph* as the 'greatest Japanese novelist of the modern period' – whose works continue to attract critical scrutiny and debate. Educated at Tokyo Imperial University, he was sent to England in 1900 as a government scholar. As one of the first Japanese writers to be influenced by Western culture, he is read by virtually all Japanese, and his influence, both on contemporary Japanese authors and throughout East Asia and beyond, has been immense.

The Tower of London

Soseki's acutely observed recollections of his experience as a Japanese scholar in Victorian London. He develops profound reflections on universal themes: the Thames is transformed into the Styx; the Tower of London becomes a gateway to the Underworld; spirits of the dead are encountered through relics and memoir.

PB / 978-0-7206-1234-9 / £14.99

'One is never in doubt that one is in the presence of greatness' – *Spectator*

The Gate

The Gate describes the everyday world of humble clerk Sosuke and his wife Oyone, a childless couple, whose quiet world is rocked first by the appearance of Sosuke's brother then the news that Oyone's estranged ex-husband will be visiting near by. Understated, poetic and profound.

PB / 978-0-7206-1250-9 / £9.95

'A sensitive, skilfully written novel' – *Guardian*

Kokoro

A meditation on the changing Japanese culture and its attitudes to honour, friendship, love and death, *Kokoro* is also a sly subversion of all these things. The novel describes the friendship between the narrator and the man he calls 'Sensei', who is haunted by mysterious events in his past until the truth is revealed in tragic circumstances.

PB / 978-0-7206-1297-4 / £9.95

'A brilliant piece of narrative' – *Spectator*

The Three-Cornered World

A painter escapes to a mountain spa to work in a world free from emotional entanglement but finds himself fascinated by the enigmatic mistress at his inn, and, inspired by thoughts of Millais' *Ophelia*, he imagines painting her. Somehow the right expression for the face eludes the artist . . .

PB / 978-0-7206-1357-5 / £9.99

'A writer to be judged by the highest standards' – *Spectator*

SHUSAKU ENDO is widely regarded as one of the greatest Japanese authors of the late twentieth century. Born in 1923, he won many major literary awards and was nominated for the Nobel Prize. As a Catholic Japanese (at a time when the Christian population of Japan was less than 1 per cent) and suffering from chronic ill health, he wrote from the perspective of the outsider. His novels, which have been translated into twenty-eight languages, include *The Sea and Poison*, *Wonderful Fool*, *Deep River*, *The Samurai*, *Scandal* and *Silence*. He died in 1996.

Silence
Endo's masterpiece, a haunting tale of tested faith, apostasy and martyrdom in feudal Japan, *Silence* follows Portuguese missionaries as they secretly travel the country to minister to the persecuted Catholic Japanese. To be filmed by Martin Scorsese.
Peter Owen Modern Classic / 978-0-7206-1286-8 / £10.95
'One of the finest historical novels written by anyone, anywhere . . . Flawless' – David Mitchell

When I Whistle
When I Whistle is a tale of the clash between new and traditional values. Set largely in a hospital, a jaded businessman, Ozu, and his doctor son are mutually contemptuous of one another's values. The story reaches a terrible climax when the son chooses to experiment on an old girlfriend of his father's with dangerous drugs.
Peter Owen Modern Classic / 978-0-7206-1437-4 / £9.99
'A most intelligent and distinguished work' – *Scotsman*

Wonderful Fool
Gaston Bonaparte, a young Frenchman visiting his pen-friend in Tokyo, is a bitter disappointment to his host, as he makes friends with street children, stray dogs, prostitutes and gangsters. Endo charts his misadventures with irony, satire and humanity.
Peter Owen Modern Classic / 978-0-7206-1320-9 / £9.95
'Endo's vision of Gaston as a Christ-like figure . . . is funny and moving.' – *Sunday Times*

The Samurai
In 1613 four Samurai set sail to bargain for a Catholic crusade through Japan in exchange for trading rights with the West. On their return they find that the Shoguns have turned against the West and are persecuting Christians. Disgraced and tormented, the Samurai begin to identify with the crucified Christ they formerly reviled.
Peter Owen Modern Classic / 978-0-7206-1185-4 / £10.95
'Genius . . . makes the imagination take wing' – *Mail On Sunday*

Scandal
An eminent Japanese-Catholic novelist is about to receive a major literary award. When a drunk woman he has never met claims she knows him well from his visits to Tokyo's red-light district, surely she must be mistaken? A dark, metaphysical and psychological thriller.
Peter Owen Modern Classic / 978-0-7206-1241-7 / £9.95
'Endo's most remarkable novel . . . a superb dramatic triumph'
– *Independent*

KAPPA
Ryunosuke Akutagawa

978-0-7206-1337-7 • PB • 141pp • £9.99

'A novel of exquisite precision'
– *Spectator*

'A classic of our times' – *Scotsman*

'A devilishly cool satire on human behaviour' – *New Statesman*

'A book with an irresistible quality . . . exquisite' – *Sunday Times*

Patient No. 23 tells his story to anyone in the asylum who will listen: on his way home through the valley he falls into a deep abyss while chasing a nimble creature with a face like a tiger and a sharp beak. It was a kappa, and when he awoke he was in Kappaland.

In the hands of Ryunosuke Akutagawa, one man's initiation into the rights of this parallel world becomes the vehicle for a savage and funny critique of Japanese life and customs in the tradition of Swift and Kafka.

A perfectly formed gem from the pen of one of Japan's most important writers, *Kappa* is at once a fable, a comedy and a brilliant satire.

RYUNOSUKE AKUTAGAWA (1892–1927) was the author of over a hundred short stories as well as translations of the works of Anatole France and Yeats. He was regarded as a major author during his lifetime, and the Akutagawa Prize, established after his suicide at the age of thirty-five, is now one of Japan's most prestigious literary awards. Two of the stories from his collection *Rashomon* formed the basis of the award-winning film of the same title by Akira Kurosawa.

SEOPYEONJE
Yi Chung-jun

Translated from the Korean by Ok Young Kim Chang

978-0-7206-1359-9 • PB • 176pp • £8.99

Yi Chung-Jun (1939–2008) is regarded as one of the most important writers of modern Korean literature. His memorable and disturbing novel *Seopyeonje* is set in the years after the Korean War in the remote south of the country, home to the traditional art of pansori, a moving and plaintively beautiful style of folk opera performed by travelling musicians. The linked stories centre on a family of itinerant singers: a boy and his step-father and half-sister. The boy believes the stepfather caused his mother's death and cannot live with the murderous hatred he feels towards him, so he disappears, leaving father and daughter to travel and perform alone. Believing her art can become elevated to the highest standards only by sensory deprivation, the father has the child blinded. Thereafter, she becomes a legendary performer throughout the region.

Years later the half-brother arrives in a village and finds his sister in a tavern. He asks her to sing for him, and with his drum accompaniment the two perform pansori throughout the night – while never explicitly acknowledging their kinship. So begins an unforgettable chain of events in one of the strangest and most haunting of novels, exploring themes such as forgiveness, the redemptive power of art and modern man's loss of innocence and alienation from traditional values – the values at the heart of this tale.

A magic-realist gem, the novel employs epic, myth and fantasy to create a fusion of the real and the fantastic. Yi Chung-Jun's story has attained near-mythical status in South Korea, especially with the acclaimed, award-winning film of the novel breaking box-office records on its release in the 1990s.
